I0718941

FIREBURN

Angela Golden Bryan

First Edition: September 2018

Printed in the United States of America

ISBN: 978-1-939237-50-7

Published by Suncoast Digital Press, Inc.
Sarasota, Florida, USA

Distributed by The Fireburn Foundation, Inc.
and Fireburn Enterprises, LLC

Cover Artwork by Allison Daigle

Contents

Dedication

For my ma,
Martha L. Golden
(1936-2018),
with love.

Foreword

by
The Honorable Myron D. Jackson, Senate President,
32nd Legislature of the Virgin Islands, St. Thomas, USVI

We all have a fire that burns within us and must be tended to. If ignored, it dies and our light goes out; if smothered, it rages within and becomes destructive; if nurtured, it brings light to all that have eyes to see. Angela Golden Bryan's screenplay, *Fireburn*, is the story of a fire that was far too long suppressed, and how one woman's erupting passion rallied a team who said, "Never again!"

This historical fiction is based on the legendary queens of the 1878 Labor Revolt in St. Croix, U.S. Virgin Islands, known as the "Fireburn." As a youth, I grew up hearing stories about the Fireburn queens, as well as many others who served as champions of civil rights and justice in the Virgin Islands. The Territory is filled with stories of determined women who not only fought for civil rights, but also for women's suffrage, thereby breaking barriers so that all could flourish.

The desperate cry of *Fireburn* resonates with any person or people whose freedom, creativity, authenticity, or passion has been squelched by others. The theme of this story empathizes with our brothers and sisters who perished in locations such as Auschwitz, Tiananmen Square, and South Africa, as well as others also persecuted for their religious beliefs, ethnicity, disabilities and gender.

"Sankofa" is the Ghanaian vernacular for an African proverb which means "go back and fetch it." This proverb teaches us that if we are to understand the who, why, and how of our present reality, it is imperative that we go back and revisit our past. It is in reclaiming our past that we are set free and can move forward. When we go back and fetch that which was left behind we can learn from our successes, and failures, thereby enabling us to plan for a better tomorrow. When we "go back and fetch it" we preserve and honor our history and culture. As a youth, "go back and fetch it" had become a guiding principle in my life without my knowing it.

As a young teen, I clearly remember the passion that swelled inside when I, along with fellow students, mounted a public campaign to preserve the architectural integrity of the historic blue bit sidewalks in the Charlotte Amalie Historic District of St. Thomas. I was a cultural preservationist before I even knew what it meant to be one. This passion has continued to grow and I have dedicated my life's work to the protection of the cultural resources and heritage of the U.S. Virgin Islands for over 30 years. I have been fortunate to serve in many official capacities directly related to my passion, such as Cultural Advisor to Governor Alexander A. Farrelly, Director of the Virgin Islands State Historic Preservation Office, and the Executive Director of the Virgin Islands Cultural Heritage Institute.

As is true of history, and a well-told story, *Fireburn* provides a valuable platform to stimulate discussions for current and future generations alike. Questions that arise are:

How can we fight injustice while rising above people and circumstances that seek to oppress us? How can we create a legacy of peace and progression without death and destruction? How can we empower, hold accountable, and work with those in positions of power and authority? How can those in authority maintain integrity and work for the good of all? How can we instill pride without fostering the oftentimes looming companion of prejudice?

As an award-winning actress, storyteller, and motivational speaker, Bryan presents dynamic characters that are relatable and evoke our love, empathy, pity, and even hatred. As one rooted in West Indian culture, Bryan's vivid descriptions ring true, making *Fireburn* a captivating read for all ages. Having spent most of my life as a servant leader dedicated to historic and cultural preservation, as well as programs designed for youth and recreation, I believe that Bryan's *Fireburn* serves as an entertaining tool to entice youth and those unfamiliar with the history, to discover our rich heritage. For those familiar with the story, *Fireburn* rekindles the memory of leaders who took a stand against unfair working conditions so similar to those held under the yoke of slavery.

Bryan's screenplay speaks to the resilience of the people, and through this fictionalized tribute pays homage to them and others who continue to pave a path forward for the Virgin Islands. *Fireburn* is an opportunity for Sankofa, and encourages the reader to go back and fetch universal lessons learned, helping create an even better future for all.

Preface

Fireburn is a call to action. The story is based on early history of St. Croix, U.S. Virgin Islands. The force for good, the courage, and the stand for human rights that immortalized the event known as "Fireburn" are more relevant today than ever.

In 2010, I was taking a storytelling course and I needed to find a good story to tell. The course textbook gave the parameters—the story should be real, emotional, truthful, simple, and valid. I was stumped and nothing came to mind. That weekend, I went to my cousin's birthday party and my aunts, Gerda and Jenny, shared family stories. I sat and listened in fascination, remembering many from my childhood days. In particular, they shared the familiar story of the Fireburn, a labor revolt that took place on the island of St. Croix back in the 1800's. I remembered hearing the story as a child, reading it in my high school Caribbean history class, and seeing it commemorated at annual celebrations.

I was mesmerized as my aunts shared how my great-great grandmother, Moriah Aaron Howell, hid herself and her younger brother and sister in a ditch, under a pile of dirt and leaves, during the revolt. I was hooked; I had to learn more and revisit the Fireburn. The more I discovered about the powerful women who led the Fireburn and how it shaped the islands' economy and entire future, the more I wanted to share the story.

I wrote a short story and began giving dramatic presentations in Toastmaster clubs, elementary schools, and women's groups. It was well-received and I won several awards. At the time, I was also an actress and I decided that

I would write a fictional screenplay based on the Fireburn. I hired a screen writing coach and envisioned having *Fireburn* filmed in the Virgin Islands, with me acting in it.

In my extensive research of the Fireburn, I found that most sources only had small blurbs dedicated to this monumental event. I also learned that, depending on who wrote the material, the "queens" in the story were described quite differently. I consulted with Senator Myron Jackson (Legislature of the U.S. Virgin Islands), an expert on the subject, and he shared helpful and factual information with me, including pictures and examples of historically-accurate women's garb for that time period. I also discovered in my research that there were actually four "queens" associated with the Fireburn, and not the three that many believed.

Although I did consult with experts and this book is based on a true event, I must state very clearly that this is not a historical document! This is a fictional screenplay inspired by history. If you are looking for a factual account of events, a history book, or a documentary, this is not for you. For others, it is my hope that you will be entertained and inspired to research the rich history of the Virgin Islands on your own, and to the extent that satisfies your curiosity. This is a fictional tribute to my ancestors presented as artists do—in their own rendition.

In addition to being a tribute to my ancestors and others who fought for what was right, I see *Fireburn* as symbolic of our passions and what we are willing to do to have them fulfilled. Figuratively speaking, there may be fields of fear and oppression that have to be burned down in order for us to rise above limitations. I am not encouraging you to literally destroy property or persons, but I am encouraging you to find your God-given passion and go for it. Align yourself with a team of likeminded people and fulfill your dreams. As Henry David Thoreau wrote, "Go confidently in the direction of your dreams! Live the life you've imagined…" As you do this, you will find that doors will open to opportunities beyond your imagination. And, as you stay true to your dreams, you will inevitably leave this world a better place than you found it.

May your personal Fireburn ignite your passion and help you rise to new heights. Fireburn!

"This is the true joy in life, the being used for a purpose recognized by yourself as a mighty one; the being a force of nature instead of a feverish, selfish little clod of ailments and grievances complaining that the world will not devote itself to making you happy.

I am of the opinion that my life belongs to the whole community, and as long as I live it is my privilege to do for it whatever I can.

I want to be thoroughly used up when I die, for the harder I work the more I live. I rejoice in life for its own sake. Life is no 'brief candle' for me. It is a sort of splendid torch which I have got hold of for the moment, and I want to make it burn as brightly as possible before handing it on to future generations."

—*George Bernard Shaw*

PART 1

MARY

EXT. ST. CROIX–ESTATE GRIFFITH–DAY–SEPTEMBER 30, 1878

Bright and sunny.

Well-manicured grounds. Expansive sugar cane fields. Luxurious plantation home.

Sweaty laborers wearily chop cane and fill donkey carts. Some laborers SING traditional gospel hymns as they work.

Teen laborer, MATHILDE "TILDA" MCBEAN, a house worker, carries a pail and offers water to laborers. They ladle water into their mouths and onto their heads.

Tilda approaches MARY THOMAS, 30's, who vigorously chops cane as though it were straw. Her "rough around the edges" facade and fierce fight for what is right often get her in trouble and hide her caring side.

Tilda stumbles on a stalk of sugar cane, falls and spills the water. Mary helps Tilda up. Tilda smooths her dress and picks up the empty pail.

Perched atop his stallion, contemptuously taking in the scene, is THOMAS GRIFFITH, 50's, the ruthless and wealthy owner of Estate Griffith. Beside him, on their steads are Griffith's ever-present puppet henchmen, WILL and JACK, 30's.

Griffith trots his horse over to Mary. Will and Jack look on. Griffith stops in front of Tilda and reaches for the whip on his holster. As he uncoils the whip, Mary defiantly steps in front of Tilda. With strength, she grabs the whip in motion. The sting of it in her hand forces her to release it. Griffith again unleashes the whip and Mary, who still stands to protect Tilda, receives a CRACK OF THE WHIP to her shoulder. Mary flinches in pain and lowers her eyes to the ground. An ugly welt forms on her shoulder.

Griffith uses the handle of his whip to lift Mary's chin, then raises the whip as though he is going to strike her again.

The BLAST of a conch shell echoes across the fields. Laborers stop their work and leave the fields, tools in hand. They walk with renewed energy, a pep in their step.

Griffith scowls, puts his whip away and looks at the laborers with an air of disdain. Griffith addresses Mary.

GRIFFITH

I will deal with you later.

Griffith's horse knocks Mary to the ground as Griffith redirects his horse, and causes the animal to rear as though he will trample Mary. Griffith LAUGHS and gallops off as Mary stares daggers at him.

INT. ESTATE GRIFFITH–STABLE–DAY

Simple wooden structure. Doors and windows open. Saddles hang neatly on the wall, tools neatly organized.

Home to several pedigree horses and a luxury carriage.

Sleeping on a bale of hay is the cantankerous, yet lovable, bespeckled driver, PAPI JACKSON, 70's. The handsome stable assistants grooming horses are half-brothers, SINGER and LEWIS PETERSON, 40's. Singer is a mulatto, without a care in the world and the darker skinned Lewis carries a horse sized chip on his shoulder.

Young, barefooted stable hands shovel manure and perform various chores.

Singer pulls a kerchief from his pocket and wipes beads of sweat on his forehead.

LEWIS

Back to work, half-breed! You're just another hired hand around here. Ah, but I almost forgot, you all can't take the heat like real men.

SINGER

Call me that one more time...

LEWIS

And what, you'll run and tell mommy like you used to when we were boys? Only mommy's not here to protect you anymore.

SINGER

No. I'll kick your backside like I used to when we were boys! And you'll run crying like you used to.

LEWIS

Yeah? In whose dream, half-breed? Mary Thomas is too much woman for you. A strong woman needs a man who can hold her, not cling to her skirt!

Enraged, Singer lunges at Lewis and knocks him to the ground. Singer gets in some good punches. Lewis gains the upper hand and pummels Singer.

The stable hands rush over and watch. Papi fans flies away as he sleeps.

A large shadow looms over the fighting men. The stable hands turn to see Griffith standing in the doorway. They fearfully scamper back to work. Singer and Lewis take notice, jump up and stand at attention.

Griffith walks over to Papi and awakens him with a nudge of his coiled whip.

> **PAPI**
> Huh? What? What's going on?

> **LEWIS**
> I was defending myself.

> **SINGER**
> Liar.

Griffith silences Singer and Lewis with a steely glare.

> **GRIFFITH**
> There are three things I hate more than anything in the world...
>
> *(to Lewis)* an uppity nigger...
>
> *(to Singer)* a thieving nigger…
>
> *(to Papi)* and a lazy nigger.

> **SINGER**
> I would never steal from you, sir.

> **GRIFFITH**
> When I pay you to take care of my stable and I come in here and catch you fighting, you are stealing.
>
> *(to Papi)*
>
> Do not come back.
>
> *(to Lewis)*

You take your ass out in the fields from now on.
You are only here because of your mother.

(*to Singer*)

Go take care of my horse.

Griffith exits the stable.

Papi sadly looks around the stable. Singer approaches him.

SINGER

I'm sorry, Papi. We could have settled this
somewhere else.

PAPI

I'm an old man. He was bound to let me go one
day. But you and Lewis have to realize what your
mother kept trying to tell you. Blood is thicker
than water.

*Lewis walks past the two men and shoves Singer with his
shoulder.*

LEWIS

You better watch your back, Whitey, we're not
done.

*Papi grabs a tattered straw hat off of a hook and leaves. Singer
tends to Griffith's horse.*

INT./EXT. ESTATE GRIFFITH–STORAGE SHACK–DAY

*Small and rustic, with dirty glass windows. Sparsely furnished
with a desk and chair. Cramped with goods. The walls are
lined with jugs of rum, wooden barrels of salted fish, burlap
bags of sugar and flour. A fat leather money pouch, ledger*

and pen rest on the desk. The door is propped open with a large stone.

A line of sweaty, dirty laborers forms outside the door. A mean looking, muscular male laborer comes from behind and moves to the front of the line, no one questions him. JONAS, 30's, the local bully, is known for picking fights.

From a distance, Mary and Tilda approach. A majestic bird soars overhead. They admire it as they walk. A gun SHOT rings out. The bird plummets and hits the ground with a soft THUD. They look in the direction of the shot and see a sneering Griffith, gun in hand.

        MARY
      That man is the devil!

Mary and Tilda step into line. Two older women follow. One fans herself with a large sea grape leaf. The other mops her face with the bottom of her apron.

Griffith sits at the desk and writes in the ledger. From the leather sack he pays each laborer. The laborers collect their wages and rations and exit.

Mary and Tilda are next.

Griffith beckons the two older women to enter ahead of Mary and Tilda. They give Mary an unsure stare.

        GRIFFITH
      Quickly—before I change my mind!

The two older women quickly enter and grab their pay and rations.

GRIFFITH (CONT'D)
Scat!

The frightened older women hastily leave. Mary enters.

GRIFFITH (CONT'D)
Uh, uh uhhh. Not so fast, Miss Mary.

Griffith points at Tilda.

GRIFFITH (CONT'D)
Her first.

Tilda hesitates.

GRIFFITH (CONT'D)
Come on now. I'm not going to bite you.

Mary nudges her forward. Tilda enters reluctantly. Griffith smiles as he slowly counts out her wages and rubs his hand on her trembling fingers. Tilda gets her rations and exits.

Griffith stands and leans on the door, arms smugly crossed while looking at Mary.

GRIFFITH (CONT'D)
As for you, you've got to pay for your insolence.

Tilda tugs Mary's arm.

TILDA
Let's go. You can have some of my food.

As Mary makes her way toward the door, Griffith grabs her arm and pulls her close.

GRIFFITH
Tell your little friend to go home.

Griffith jabs Mary with his gun.

MARY
Tilda, go home.

Tilda does not move. Mary gives Tilda a warning look.

TILDA
But...

MARY
We all have to eat and you have your own mouths to feed.

Tilda glances back as she leaves. Griffith leers at Mary.

GRIFFITH
And I have to eat too. Lucky for you, I like my food spicy.

Griffith grabs Mary's shoulder in the same spot that he whipped her. Mary flinches in pain. He shoves her into the shack and bolts the door.

EXT. DIRT ROAD–DAY

Lined with thick tropical foliage on either side.

Tilda walks with rations in hand, turns a corner and spots Papi a few yards away.

TILDA
Papi! Papi! Wait up!

Papi acknowledges Tilda. She catches up with him.

PAPI
Where's Mary?

TILDA
Getting her rations.

PAPI
So long?

Tilda nods her head and looks straight ahead. Papi touches her arm.

PAPI (CONT'D)
What's wrong?

TILDA
Nothing, she's coming soon.

Realization floods Papi's face and he quickly turns and heads back in the direction from which they came, Tilda follows.

TILDA (CONT'D)
Where are you going?

PAPI
I will kill him dead!

TILDA
No, Papi, please! He will kill you.

Papi hobbles down the road, Tilda in tow. Papi's stride slows, and he leans against a tree. Tilda quickly settles him on the ground beneath the tree.

TILDA

Papi. You're not as young as you used to be. What are you going to do? Griffith will kill you and laugh about it to Mary.

Papi does not respond. He takes several deep breaths and looks toward the sky. He taps Tilda to help him up and finally responds.

PAPI

Well, I will die doing the right thing!

INT. STORAGE SHACK–DAY

Bent over the desk is a stoic Mary. She smooths her skirt down as Griffith buckles his belt and places his holster with whip and gun around his waist.

Griffith grabs a jug of rum, uncorks it and takes a swig.

GRIFFITH

Damn good rum!

Griffith rips a bag of flour open and pours it on the floor. He dumps salted fish on top. He spits on it, then points to the pile.

GRIFFITH (CONT'D)

Don't forget your rations.

Griffith unlocks the door and exits.

Mary peers into the empty salt fish barrel. Her skirt hem catches on a sharp piece of metal and rips.

Mary approaches the door and glances back at the pile of flour and fish on the floor. She quickly grabs a bag and scrapes the flour and fish into it.

INT. ESTATE GRIFFITH–KITCHEN–DAY

Spacious and bright. Large wooden work table in center with shiny pots hanging above, potbelly stove in corner. Large, well-stocked pantry.

The matronly yet voluptuous cook, SUSANNA "BOTTOM BELLY" ABRAHAMSEN, 40's, CHUCKLES as she inspects the contents of Mary's bag. Mary leaves, empty handed, in triumph.

EXT. DIRT ROAD–DAY

Mary walks briskly, heading away from Estate Griffith. She spots Papi and Tilda in the distance and yells.

> **MARY**
> Papi! Tilda!

Tilda runs and embraces Mary. Papi hobbles faster. Papi holds her at arm's length and inspects her.

> **PAPI**
> You alright?

> **MARY**
> Of course I'm alright, that's a silly question.

Papi looks at Tilda and then back at Mary. They walk.

MARY (CONT'D)
I hope Tilda hasn't been filling your head with lies again.

PAPI
I will kill him. Kill him dead!

MARY
Yeah? You and whose army?

PAPI
I still have some fight left in me.

MARY
Is that how you got fired?

PAPI
People don't know how to mind their own business.

MARY
You should talk! You always know all the melee.

PAPI
Woman, hush up and walk!

MARY
Those two idiots cost you your job with their constant fighting!

PAPI
Well, I was sleeping.

MARY

Still, they should know better. Always bickering about one thing or another. You're lucky I still have my job.

PAPI

I don't need no damn woman taking care of me! I'll get a job at the new Central Sugar Factory.

MARY

The sugar factory?

PAPI

The boys said the factory is looking for workers. And they pay thirty cents a week–not this stinking ten cents!

MARY

Yeah?

TILDA

It must be true. Papi is like the town news.

MARY

Yes, he's a nosy old man.

PAPI

Nosy or not, they'll hire me.

Papi pulls a small, gold hoop earring from his pant pocket and waves it in front of Mary's face. Mary rolls her eyes and Tilda LAUGHS.

> **PAPI (CONT'D)**
> General Buddhoe took this from his ear and—

Mockingly, Mary takes over Papi's speech.

> **MARY**
> —and gave it to me after he helped end slavery. He told me that it will give me luck and help conquer armies.

> **PAPI**
> Oh, so you do listen to me.

> **MARY**
> Hmph! Where was the good luck a few hours ago?

> **PAPI**
> That was good luck! I've been trying to leave that place for years. You need to leave too.

> **MARY**
> If I had a choice, I'd have left a long time ago.

A village of dilapidated shacks comes into view.

Mary and Tilda turn off the dirt road in the direction of the shacks. Papi hesitates.

Papi's look goes from pensive to excited. He kisses his earring and puts it back in his pocket.

> **PAPI**
> Come with me, Mary. You wouldn't let an old man go to the factory by himself, would you?

MARY

I thought you didn't need any woman's help.

PAPI

Can't you take a joke?

Mary, arms folded, not budging.

PAPI (CONT'D)

I'll give you a sip of my guavaberry rum.

Mary raises her eyebrows in interest.

MARY

Three sips.

PAPI

Two.

Mary LAUGHS and Tilda goes her separate way.

Tilda makes her way toward the shacks as Papi and Mary continue down the road.

The SOUND OF A CARRIAGE. Papi and Mary look behind. Singer is driving a luxurious carriage. He stops and tips his hat at Papi and Mary.

SINGER

Good afternoon, Papi, Mary.

Mary continues walking. Papi stops and GREETS Singer.

PAPI
You make a fine driver, Singer. You remind me of myself when I was your age.

SINGER
I feel bad about what happened.

PAPI
I'm an old man, Singer, it was time.

Mary stops and faces them.

MARY
You should feel bad!

SINGER
At least let me give you a ride.

PAPI
Thank you.

Singer stands and assists Papi into the carriage.

MARY
Papi, you can't let him get away with this so easy!

Mary runs to the carriage and pulls Papi's arm. Papi shakes Mary off as he climbs into the carriage.

Singer offers his hand to Mary. She walks away. He slowly drives the carriage alongside her.

SINGER
Come on, get in.

MARY

My legs are just fine.

SINGER

I can see that. You afraid I'm going to bite you?

MARY

I wish your mangy rass would try to bite me, I'll knock your teeth out of your mouth!

Singer LAUGHS heartily. Papi CHUCKLES.

SINGER

Cheese and bread, man! You must have had a hard day.

Mary eyes Singer suspiciously.

SINGER (CONT'D)

Can't a man be generous?

MARY

Generosity has a price.

SINGER

In your world.

With a look of disbelief, Singer commands the horse to TROT, leaving Mary behind.

Papi leans over to Singer.

PAPI

Stop the carriage.

The carriage stops.

PAPI (CONT'D)

Not one more word from you, woman. Get in!

Mary strides defiantly to the carriage. Singer extends his hand to her. She refuses it and climbs into the carriage. While Mary is still standing, Singer jerks the carriage forward and Mary falls onto the seat.

Singer stifles a smile. Papi looks at each of them and shakes his head. Mary fumes.

EXT. CENTRAL SUGAR FACTORY–DAY

The white, new building stands tall and proud. The windows are clean and shiny. A freshly painted sign hangs at the entrance "CENTRAL SUGAR FACTORY".

A group of mostly male laborers (various ages) crowd in front of the building. Among the group are Lewis and Jonas.

Standing next to them is BIG MAN, 20's, a massive mute laborer. He quietly takes in the scene.

Singer stops the carriage, Papi and Mary dismount.

PAPI

God bless you, Singer.

Mary turns away. Papi SCOLDS her.

PAPI (CONT'D)

Don't you have any manners in your mouth, gal?

Mary grudgingly turns to Singer, avoiding eye contact.

MARY

Thank you.

SINGER

At your service, ma'am.

Mary and Papi head to the back of the crowd. Precocious CY, (9), one of the laborer's sons approaches. Mary and Cy embrace.

CY

Good afternoon, Miss Mary.

MARY

Aren't you a little young to be looking for a job here?

CY

Age doesn't matter.

PAPI

That's right!

The crowd grows.

INT. CENTRAL SUGAR FACTORY–HIMMELMAN'S OFFICE–DAY

Clean, well-lit.

Looking out the window is ERNST HIMMELMAN, 40's, the CEO of the factory who puts justice before greed. A large foreman stands next to him.

INT. HIMMELMAN MANSION – EVENING

Spacious and extravagant. A newspaper rests on a table. Headline reads "Nancy Himmelman, Wife of Prominent Businessman Dies."

A young boy, HIMMELMAN, cries as various people, dressed in black, solemnly leave the home.

A matronly black woman closes the door, and heads to the room where young Himmelman sits. A man pours a drink and plops into a chair, paying no attention to the boy. The woman approaches the man.

> **BLACK WOMAN**
> Sir, I can take Ernst with me tonight.

The man does not answer. The woman waits a few seconds before leaving with the boy.

INT. BLACK WOMAN'S SHACK – NIGHT

Small, poorly lit, well-kept. The black woman and the boy enter.

> **YOUNG HIMMELMAN**
> Who's going to be my mother now?

> **BLACK WOMAN**
> As long as your father lets me, I'll take care of you.

She embraces him and gently strokes his head.

INT. CENTRAL SUGAR FACTORY–HIMMELMAN'S OFFICE–DAY

> **HIMMELMAN**
> I wish I could hire them all.

> **FOREMAN**
> Twenty, sir?

Himmelman nods "yes."

> **HIMMELMAN**
> This building will bring dignity to the Negroes.
> They will have a safe place to work and fair wages.

—COURTYARD

The foreman selects twenty of the biggest and strongest looking men, including Lewis. He passes over Jonas, Cy, Papi, all of the women and smaller men. He passes over Big Man. MURMURING in the crowd.

> **JONAS**
> I'm stronger than any one of them.

> **FOREMAN**
> No troublemakers here! Everyone–go home.

Jonas shoves past the foreman.

> **MARY**
> What about Big Man? Just because he can't talk is
> no reason not to pick him.

FOREMAN
I have a job to do.

Papi steps up and points at Mary.

PAPI
And what about her?

The foreman ignores Papi.

PAPI (CONT'D)
Oh, I see what's going on. You must want all those strong young bucks for yourself.

The foreman angrily lunges at Papi and pushes him.

FOREMAN
I'm not a damn antiman!

Papi falls.

Enraged, Mary jumps on the foreman's back and pummels him. The foreman tries to shake loose. The crowd CHEERS the fight on. Two laborers place bets.

MARY
That's no way to treat an old man!

Cy helps Papi off the ground and brushes him off. Papi MUMBLES.

PAPI
I had it under control!

Himmelman comes face to face with the foreman and Mary.

HIMMELMAN
What is going on?

Mary slides off the foreman's back.

FOREMAN
Sir, this woman—

PAPI
—this woman, Mary, is smarter than any one of those big bucks he chose, and she's strong.

Papi pulls a kerchief from his pants pocket and wipes sweat from his brow.

HIMMELMAN
"Mary" is it?

MARY
Yes, sir.

HIMMELMAN
Your father says you are strong and smart. What do you have to say for yourself?

MARY
I can read, sir. The Moravian missionaries taught me.

Himmelman looks around, points to the sign on the building.

> **HIMMELMAN**
> Read that sign.

Mary slowly sounds out the words.

> **MARY**
> Central Sugar Factory.

> **HIMMELMAN**
> Good.

Himmelman is quiet for a moment. He spots a wheelbarrow with a bag of sugar in it.

> **HIMMELMAN (CONT'D)**
> Wheel that barrel to me.

Mary walks over to the wheelbarrow, lifts it up and drops it.

> **HIMMELMAN (CONT'D)**
> Don't fret, it's heavy.

Mary walks over to a pile of bagged sugar, laboriously picks one up and adds it to the wheelbarrow. She wheels both bags of sugar painstakingly over to him, sweat beads her forehead. The crowd CHANTS her name.

> **HIMMELMAN (CONT'D)**
> It looks like you have yourself a job, Mary. And Big Man too. See you both after Contract Day.

EXT./INT. ESTATE GRIFFITH–NIGHT

Uniformed drivers park carriages. Elegantly dressed guests dismount.

Standing in the plush foyer, greeting guests, are Griffith and his wife.

Guests make their way down the corridor. Men head for Griffith's study and women head for the parlor where they sip tea and GOSSIP.

—GRIFFITH'S STUDY

The men admire Griffith's extensive gun collection.

Griffith addresses the people-pleasing, rotund and sweaty governor of the island, AUGUST GARDE, 60's.

> **GRIFFITH**
> What type of trouble, sir?

> **GOVERNOR GARDE**
> My commander tells me there's more complaining than usual. Never a good sign before Contract Day.

Tilda serves the men drinks.

> **GRIFFITH**
> Your soldiers are fresh from Denmark and do not understand that this year is no different, laborers always want more. The bastards are lucky. We give them a house, food and even land to grow their provisions on.

HIMMELMAN
Since when does hard work constitute luck?

Griffith dismisses Himmelman's remark.

GRIFFITH
Besides, we cannot give them more wages
or rations because of the damn sugar beets
competing with our sugar cane. They will have to
wait until next year's Contract Day.

HIMMELMAN
There's plenty of sugar being made every day, Mr.
Griffith, which means crops continue to do well.

GRIFFITH
How long have you been on the island, Mr.
Himmelman? A year? Two?

HIMMELMAN
Long enough to know that slavery was abolished
over 30 years ago and these "lucky" people, as you
put it, are still being treated like slaves.

Several men glance uneasily at Griffith and Himmelman.

GRIFFITH
Gentlemen, please forgive Mr. Himmelman. He
doesn't quite understand the natural order of
things here in the Danish West Indies.

HIMMELMAN
Treating human beings unjustly can hardly be
considered natural.

GRIFFITH

From the beginning of time, there has always been an inferior race, destined to serve the superior. It's no different here. The Negroes on this island are here to assist those like you and me in creating wealth. In exchange, we give them food, shelter and wages. They don't have the same tastes that we have, so their needs are different.

Trust me, you don't want to get caught in the middle of trying to change the natural rhythm of life. This is a dance we must always lead in.

Governor Garde, cluelessly pipes in.

GOVERNOR GARDE

I can hardly wait to taste the feast Susanna has prepared this year. The Negroes are gifted chefs!

—DINING ROOM

Large dining table overflowing with gourmet delicacies and fine china.

CLINKING sounds of dinnerware and silverware as the guests eat. Soft MURMUR of conversation.

Uniformed servants attend to guests, while others stand at attention.

At the head of the table sits Griffith.

Griffith stands and CLINKS his wine glass with his knife.

GRIFFITH

I would like to propose a toast.

Guests raise their glasses.

GRIFFITH (CONT'D)
We drink to another successful Contract Day!

Himmelman reluctantly raises his glass, as the other guests toast Griffith enthusiastically. Griffith sits and returns to his conversation with the governor.

GOVERNOR GARDE
Name your price. Give Susanna to me and I will pay your price and give you my cook and her daughter.

GRIFFITH
That might be a deal for me if either one of them could cook.

Both men LAUGH raucously at Griffith's humorous refusal.

GOVERNOR GARDE
The least you can do is call her in so I can compliment the chef.

GRIFFITH
I will make sure she gets the message.

GOVERNOR GARDE
I would like to tell her myself.

Griffith turns to one of the uniformed servants.

GRIFFITH
Bring Susanna in here.

Susanna enters and stands obediently in front of the governor.

SUSANNA

Yes, sir?

GOVERNOR GARDE

Your cooking is a taste of heaven!

SUSANNA

Thank you, sir.

The governor points to a piece of food that Griffith is cutting and eating.

GOVERNOR GARDE

What are those? They are divine.

SUSANNA

Salt fish fritters, sir.

GRIFFITH

My favorite.

SUSANNA

Yes, sir. One of the laborers wanted to make sure Mr. Griffith had his favorite meal tonight and donated all of her rations for the fritters.

GOVERNOR GARDE

Well now that just shows you've got a good handle on your plantation.

GRIFFITH

Who, Susanna?

SUSANNA
Pardon me, sir?

GRIFFITH
Who donated their rations?

SUSANNA
Mary Thomas, sir.

Griffith places his forkful of uneaten food on his plate and pushes his plate away.

GRIFFITH
You are excused, Susanna.

Susanna gives a quick nod and leaves.

GOVERNOR GARDE
Mighty fine Negroes you've got working for you. You have got to make sure you reward that Negress of yours.

GRIFFITH
Oh, I will, Governor. Mary Thomas will get everything that she deserves.

EXT. LABORERS' QUARTERS–NIGHT

Tiny, dilapidated wooden shacks line a narrow dirt road.

An open area serves as a barbecue pit with a skewered pig roasting over an open fire. Surrounding the pit are large logs which serve as seats.

A few yards away is a cistern, and a wooden bucket.

Seated around the fire, drinking rum and CHATTING loudly, are Papi and other male laborers. The mood is festive.

Singer and five other men form a scratch band. They use drums and conch shells to make calypso MUSIC.

Lewis watches from afar.

Tilda and several teen girls tend to the children. Some children watch hermit crabs race. Others run around, climb trees and play games.

—OUTDOOR MAKESHIFT KITCHEN

The women cook traditional West Indian fare in pots and pans that sit on top of hot coal pots. Swirls of smoke fill the air.

Mary pulls a pouch of seasoning from her apron and seasons fish by cutting "x's" into them and rubbing the seasoning into the cut. Fish are piled onto a large banana tree leaf.

Kneading dough in a large calabash bowl is AXELINE SALOMON, 30's, sexy and curvaceous.

A figures approaches Mary and Axeline. It is Susanna, with a large bag in hand.

>   **SUSANNA**
> Wait until you see the goodies we got this year.

>   **MARY**
> Just as long as it's not salt fish fritters!

Mary and Susanna LAUGH.

>   **AXELINE**
> I love salt fish fritters.

MARY

Trust me, Axeline, you wouldn't want any of these.

Susanna continues to CHUCKLE as Axeline stares at her. Mary places the seasoned fish on a sizzling hot skillet.

SUSANNA

(to Axeline)

If you don't pay attention you're going to burn yourself. Or worst yet, burn the Johnnycakes.

AXELINE

Okay then, you come and do it since you're the famous "Cookie."

SUSANNA

Move, gal. I don't know why Mary even let you touch the food.

Susanna takes over. Axeline saunters over to a nearby tree and stares in the direction of the scratch band. She SIGHS longingly.

MARY

(to Axeline)

What, or should I say "who", has your attention tonight?

AXELINE

Isn't it obvious?

SUSANNA

I'm not even going to ask because tomorrow it will be somebody else.

AXELINE

This time it's different. I can tell by the way he's been looking at me all night.

Mary and Susanna look at the band. The band members are playing and Singer is SINGING.

MARY

Nobody is looking at you, Axeline.

AXELINE

Just wait, you'll see.

—AROUND THE OPEN PIT

Everyone is eating. The older people sit on the logs while children and younger adults sit on the ground. A few stand.

The food is served on banana leaves and everyone uses their fingers to eat with. No food is wasted.

Papi sucks the eyes out of the fish's head and cleans every piece of meat out of it.

CY

(to his mother)

Can I have more kallaloo, please?

Cy's Mother, MARTHA, looks at her empty cup.

MARTHA

It's finished.

Mary stops eating.

> **MARY**
> I'm so full! Cy, come help me eat this food.

Cy approaches Mary, hands outstretched, ready to take the offered kallaloo. Martha gives Cy a warning look. Cy withdraws his hands.

> **MARY (CONT'D)**
> The food will waste if he doesn't eat it.

Mary hands Cy her cup.

> **CY**
> Thank you, Miss Mary.

Martha smiles thankfully at Mary.

—OUTDOOR MAKESHIFT KITCHEN

Mary, Susanna, Axeline and other women clean up and wash pots.

Singer CROONS a love song. His look lingers on Mary. The men drink and CHAT and the children play.

Mary takes several clean pots back to her shack.

Axeline sits, being of little help, as she dreamily looks at Singer.

> **AXELINE**
> Singer can't take his eyes off of me.

Susanna looks in the direction of the band. Singer glances in their direction briefly and then scans the crowd, as though he is looking for someone.

SUSANNA
Are you sure it's you he's looking at?

AXELINE
Who else would it be?

SUSANNA
Singer's a good man. Leave him alone.

AXELINE
And I'm a good woman.

SUSANNA
You know what I mean.

AXELINE
You must want him for yourself. Are you jealous?

Mary approaches Susanna and Axeline.

MARY
Who's jealous?

AXELINE
I was just telling Susanna that Singer is all mine. I think she wants him for herself.

Mary looks surprised. Axeline turns to face the band and SQUEALS in delight.

> **AXELINE (CONT'D)**
> See! He's looking at me again.

Susanna and Mary notice Singer looking in their direction, smiling. Axeline smiles. Mary addresses Axeline sarcastically.

> **MARY**
> I guess this is your lucky day.

Susanna walks away. Mary roughly scrubs a pot.

Axeline seductively sways her hips as she approaches the band. Singer stops SINGING as Axeline whispers in his ear. Singer gives a small smile and Axeline walks away. She coyly glances back at Singer who is SINGING again.

Mary inconspicuously watches Singer and Axeline as she scrubs the pot.

Susanna approaches Mary.

> **SUSANNA**
> You're going to bore a hole in that pot! I'll finish. Why don't you get some water to put out the fire?

Mary MUMBLES and glances at Singer.

> **MARY**
> Which fire?

Susanna gives a knowing smile.

> **SUSANNA**
> What?

MARY
>> Nothing.

Mary hastily heads to the cistern and fills the bucket with water.

Singer continues to CROON a tune. As Mary passes by he gently touches her arm.

Mary, taken aback, throws the bucket of water on Singer. Everyone LAUGHS at the shocked expression on Singer's face. Singer calmly wipes his face with his hands.

Lewis leans against a tree and takes in the scene from a distance.

PAPI
>> You better watch out. That one is hot like pepper!

SINGER
>> I think she likes me.

The band members LAUGH as well as Papi and other laborers.

In a huff, Mary quickly strides back to the coal pot and tosses the remaining water on the hot coals. There isn't much water left and the coals smoke and SIZZLE. Mary looks at the empty bucket then looks over at the cistern. She doesn't budge.

Susanna extends her hand to Mary and Mary gives her the bucket.

SUSANNA
>> I'm not even going to ask.

Susanna goes to the cistern. Mary walks over to her shack and sits on the steps of her porch, watching the festivities.

The band PLAYS a lively song and many people dance.

Lewis approaches and leans against the porch, facing Mary.

LEWIS
I'm sorry about Papi losing his job. Singer started everything and I had to defend myself.

MARY
There's three sides to that story. Yours, his, and the truth.

LEWIS
I saw what you just did. You know his character.

MARY
Do I?

LEWIS
Marry me.

MARY
Where did that come from?

LEWIS
We are the same, and now you're going to need help since Papi doesn't have a job.

MARY
Oh, so you do charity work now?

LEWIS

Call me Father Lewis.

MARY

And what do you get out of this, Father Lewis?

LEWIS

A good wife.

MARY

You must think I'm stupid. You men are all the same!

LEWIS

Call me crazy for even trying. You make it real hard for a man.

MARY

Okay, crazy Father Lewis.

LEWIS

So, you will marry me?

Mary LAUGHS.

MARY

Misson, you move too quick for me.

LEWIS

Your life would be easier, Mary.

MARY

I have never seen a man make a woman's life easier.

LEWIS

I promise you that will be my goal, every minute of the day. Think about it.

MARY

Good night, Lewis.

Lewis tips his head to Mary and leaves.

BAND MEMBER

(sings)

General Buddhoe helped free the slaves in 1848. Everybody knows he wasn't a minute too late. So today we can sing, we are free, we are free, thank God we are free! We are free, we are free, thank God we are free!

The crowd joins in the CHORUS "We are free, we are free, thank God we are free!"

Mary listens from her porch, suddenly jumps up and storms over to the band.

MARY

How can you sing about being free when we are still hungry?

Cy leans over to his mother.

CY

I thought she was full.

MARTHA

Shhh!

MARY

How can you say we are free when they still beat us and use us whenever they want? This is just slavery by another name!

Stunned looks from the crowd.

MARY (CONT'D)

This is exactly how they want us. Drunk and too stupid to think. You might as well stay home and not go to Contract Day tomorrow because, mark my words, nothing will change!

PAPI

She's right! What would Buddhoe do if he was here?

BAND MEMBER

He'd sit his backside down and have another drink!

LAUGHTER from the crowd.

MARY

Papi, it's useless, don't waste your breath.

SINGER

Who would lead us?

PAPI

I will!

More LAUGHTER from the crowd.

PAPI (CONT'D)

We could get workers from all the plantations to join up with us. That's how Buddhoe did it. They were 8000 strong!

BAND MEMBER

Are you looking for a fight, old man? Okay, let's fight.

The band member affectionately roughhouses with Papi. Papi's good luck earring falls from his pocket to the dirt, he does not notice.

Frustrated, Mary walks away. Singer follows. The music PLAYS in the background.

SINGER

Maybe you should do something.

Mary SUCKS HER TEETH at Singer and turns to leave. Singer stops her.

SINGER (CONT'D)

You're the one ranting and raving about freedom. The fire for it shoots from your eyes.

MARY

Singer, what we really need is somebody like Buddhoe.

SINGER
Buddhoe is dead. But here you stand, alive and well,
and strong. If you want freedom Mary, take it.

Singer returns to the band.

EXT./INT. MARY'S SHACK – DAY

—CONTRACT DAY – OCTOBER 1, 1878

*Small vegetable garden. Clothesline made with frayed rope
and old wooden beams. Bush tea boils in a pot on top of a
coal pot.*

A rooster CROWS.

*Mary enters the sparsely furnished shack and places a chipped
enamel plate topped with roasted saltfish and fungi on the
table.*

Papi sits on the edge of his cot, head hung over.

MARY
Good morning, Papi.

PAPI
Stop yelling!

Papi slowly gets up and shuffles over to the table and sits.

MARY
Nobody's yelling around here except you.

PAPI
Oh Lord, help me!

> **MARY**
> Why should the Lord help you when you drank one week's worth of rum in one night? You never learn!

Mary sits at the table and makes the sign of the cross before eating.

> **MARY (CONT'D)**
> You going to eat?

> **PAPI**
> I need to drink my tea first. Where's the sugar?

> **MARY**
> It's finished.

> **PAPI**
> We didn't get any yesterday with the rations?

Mary shakes her head "No". Papi BANGS his fist on the table.

> **PAPI (CONT'D)**
> It starts today!

> **MARY**
> What does?

Papi has renewed vigor and purpose.

> **PAPI**
> Us making Buddhoe proud.

MARY

Us? Don't drag me into your crazy plans.

PAPI

You got me to thinking last night. Thirty years after freedom was "bolished" and we're still living like this.

MARY

Things will be better after I start working at the factory.

PAPI

It's not just about us.

Mary gets up and clears away her dishes. Papi TALKS between bites of food.

MARY

It is. That's why you shouldn't even go to Contract Day. Nothing will change.

PAPI

You're wrong, gal. I have a good feeling about today! I have a piece of Buddhoe's spirit right here.

Papi pats his pants pocket and frantically searches it.

PAPI (CONT'D)

Oh, sweet Jesus…no, no, no!

Mary picks up a small, tattered throw rug.

MARY
You alright?

PAPI
Where's Buddhoe's earring?

MARY
Don't look at me.

PAPI
It's you—you thieved it just so I'd stay home!
Me and Momma should have left you on the
wharf when you got to the island and didn't have
anybody.

Mary is stunned and hurt.

PAPI (CONT'D)
Oh God help me. Things won't go well unless I
have Buddhoe's earring.

Mary storms out of the house with the rug.

*Chickens CLUCK and scratch for food. They scatter as Mary
angrily throws the rug over the clothesline and beats it with a
broom.*

Susanna and her family approach on foot.

SUSANNA
You trying to kill that rug?

Mary continues to beat the rug.

SUSANNA (CONT'D)
Papi talking crazy again?

Mary stops and nods her head.

MARY
He needs a good thump on his head!

SUSANNA
And sometimes so do you. Hurry up, we want a good spot!

MARY
Go on, I'm not stopping you.

SUSANNA
You're not coming?

MARY
I have work to do.

SUSANNA
You're missing Contract Day to beat a rug?

Papi comes outside, he looks sad.

SUSANNA (CONT'D)
Good morning, Papi.

Papi GRUNTS.

SUSANNA (CONT'D)
Papi, you look like you lost your best friend.

PAPI
I did.

SUSANNA
Don't worry, you and Mary will make up soon.
You always do.

PAPI
I'm not talking about Mary! It's Buddhoe. He's gone.

SUSANNA
Papi, he's been gone for 30 years.

PAPI
I know that! Somebody thieved Buddhoe's earring
and now I can't feel his spirit anymore.

SUSANNA
Why do you need to feel his spirit?

PAPI
To fight the battle.

*Susanna gives Mary a questioning look. Mary throws up her
hands, resigned, and goes back to beating the rug.*

PAPI (CONT'D)
Let's go before the sun gets too hot!

*Susanna, her family and Papi leave. Mary MUMBLES under
her breath.*

MARY
Crazy old man.

EXT. ESTATE GRIFFITH–DAY

—PORCH

Griffith's wife and other women sit and drink tea while young mulatto children fan them.

—GROUNDS

Griffith, Himmelman, Governor Garde and other plantation owners skeet shoot. Tilda stands next to a tray filled with glasses of water.

HIMMELMAN
The militia, in full force? Is that not a bit extreme for a Contract Day gathering?

GOVERNOR GARDE
Rumors have it that the Negroes are extra feisty this year. The Commander of the Fort thought it would be important to make a statement.

GRIFFITH
Yes, he is a wise man.

GOVERNOR GARDE
Under my direction, of course.

GRIFFITH
Of course.

GOVERNOR GARDE
And I said to him, "Commander, if there is any trouble, carry out my orders!"

HIMMELMAN
What might those orders be, sir?

The governor takes his time and aims his gun.

GOVERNOR GARDE
For anyone making trouble...

The governor YELLS.

GOVERNOR GARDE (CONT'D)
Pull!

Governor Garde SHATTERS the clay plate with one shot. Griffith is pleased.

EXT. MARY'S SHACK–DAY

Mary weeds her vegetable garden. Out of breath and sweating, Tilda runs up to Mary.

MARY
Slow down, gal.

TILDA
They're going to shoot people!

MARY

Who is shooting who?

Tilda's mother, father, younger brother and sister rush to her.

TILDA'S FATHER

What's wrong?

TILDA

The governor told the soldiers to shoot anybody that's making trouble. Shoot them dead!

TILDA'S MOTHER

Are you making up stories again, Tilda?

TILDA

No, ma'am.

MARY

Who told you this?

TILDA

I heard it when I was giving the men water.

TILDA'S FATHER

Let's go! Mary, you coming?

MARY

No. Go ahead.

Tilda and family leave. Mary returns to her weeding.

EXT. FORT FREDERIK–DAY

The impressive red brick structure sits along the waterfront, cannons aimed toward the sea. A grassy lawn surrounds a white, gazebo style bandstand. Horses and carriages are parked along the street.

Hundreds of laborers are gathered. Some sell food. Some mill about and TALK, others sit on the grass and eat. Martha is frying beignets on a small coal pot. Cy helps her.

Plantation owners and overseers group together around the bandstand.

Armed soldiers patrol. Some on foot, some on horses.

EXT. MARY'S SHACK–DAY

Mary looks up from her weeding and sees a chicken pecking at a small shiny object in the dirt. She goes to investigate. It is Papi's earring. She shoos the chicken and picks it up.

Mary stares at the earring and gives an exasperated SIGH.

> **MARY**
> Crazy old man!

Mary sticks the earring in her skirt pocket and runs toward the dirt road.

EXT. FORT FREDERIK–DAY

The crowd of laborers continues to grow.

A drunk laborer attracts attention when he CHANTS and waves his rum bottle in the air.

DRUNK LABORER
Contract Day–we want more pay!

Two patrolling soldiers take notice of the drunk laborer and approach. The drunk laborer sees them and staggers off. The soldiers follow him.

Laborers look on.

The drunk laborer stumbles and falls. His bottle of rum falls also. Soldier 1 roughly picks him up. As the drunk laborer reaches for his rum bottle Soldier 1 SMASHES it with the butt of his rifle.

SOLDIER 1
You have had enough.

The drunk laborer bends over and picks up a piece of the broken bottle and examines it. Disappointed, he turns to face the soldier and raises the broken shard as he WHINES.

DRUNK LABORER
You broke my rum...

Soldier 1 hits the drunk laborer in the face with the butt of his rifle. The drunk laborer collapses, blood oozing from his nose.

The drunk laborer feebly raises the broken shard and CRIES.

DRUNK LABORER (CONT'D)
...you broke it.

SOLDIER 2
Why did you do that? He is just a drunk.

SOLDIER 1
You saw him. He tried to attack me with that broken bottle!

The crowd MURMURS their displeasure.

SOLDIER 1 (CONT'D)
Alright everyone, back to what you were doing and there will not be any trouble!

Someone in the crowd throws a rock which hits Soldier 1 in the head. Papi is jostled and his glasses fall off his face. He bends over to pick them up.

Soldier 1 looks around and sees Papi picking something up. As Papi stands, Soldier 1 shoots Papi. Papi clutches his stomach and falls.

Laborers SCREAM in fear. Chaos ensues. Several laborers surround the two soldiers and beat them. Other laborers throw sticks and stones at nearby soldiers and planters.

The COMMANDER OF THE FORT, 50's, FIRES his gun into the air.

COMMANDER OF THE FORT
Attack!

Soldiers beat laborers with clubs and fire shots into the crowd.

Mary hears the screams as she approaches and picks up her pace. She sees the chaos and runs into the crowd, eyes searching desperately.

A bag of beignets is knocked from Cy's hand. As he tries to gather them up, people trample them and knock him over.

He notices Papi lying on the ground, a few yards away being trampled. He abandons the beignets and rushes over to Papi.

Cy laboriously pulls Papi to a nearby tree and leans Papi against it.

CY
Papi, I'm going to find Mary.

Papi clutches his stomach, blood oozing from his wound. He feebly nods his head.

Cy runs off and looks around, as though searching for someone. He spots Mary in the distance. He rushes over to her.

CY (CONT'D)
They shot Papi!

MARY
Oh God, please no!

Cy grabs Mary's hand and runs. He leads her to the tree where he had left Papi. Papi is not there. They look around frantically. Singer is carrying Papi to a nearby quiet alley. Mary and Cy run after Singer.

As Singer gently places Papi on the ground, Susanna quickly approaches with wads of white cloth and a small bottle of rum.

She rips Papi's shirt open and gently presses the cloth against his wound. The cloth quickly becomes bloodstained. She gives Papi a swig of the rum and he COUGHS. Papi closes his eyes.

Mary holds back tears as she sits and cradles Papi's head on her lap. Papi looks at her.

PAPI
Buddhoe?

MARY
No Papi, it's me, Mary.

PAPI
Buddhoe, wait for me, I'm coming.

MARY
I have something for you, Papi.

Mary pulls the gold earring out of her pocket and hands it to Papi. Papi CHUCKLES and COUGHS.

PAPI
I knew it would come back to me.

Papi slowly turns his head and appears to be talking to someone.

PAPI (CONT'D)
Yes, sir. Thank you, sir.

After a few seconds of silence, Papi reaches for Mary's hands and places the earring in her hand. He folds her fingers over it and holds her hand. Mary shakes her head "no," refusing to take it.

PAPI (CONT'D)
Buddhoe said it's time to pass it on.

MARY

What are you talking about, old man? You have work to do...

Papi slumps in Mary's arms. Mary stares at Papi in disbelief and clings to the earring.

Susanna steps forward and reassuringly rests her hand on Mary's shoulder. They are all silent for a moment. Mary reaches into Papi's pocket and takes a wide kerchief from it. She ties it around her head. Cy and Singer look on.

Tilda and her mother drag Tilda's father out of the crowd, his leg is bleeding. Tilda's brother and sister are CRYING.

TILDA'S FATHER

(To Tilda)

Take the children and hide.

TILDA

I can't...

TILDA'S MOTHER

Take them now! Run!

TILDA'S FATHER

Don't come out until everything is quiet.

Tilda nods her head. Her brother and sister cling to their mother. Their mother peels them off of her and gives them to Tilda.

TILDA

But...

TILDA'S FATHER
Hush up, gal! Go now.

Tilda grabs her brother and sister by the hands and runs to a nearby ditch and covers them and herself with garbage, dirt and leaves. Tilda holds and comforts them as they all lie down and hide in silence.

EXT./INT. WAREHOUSE–DAY

Medium sized, wooden and functional. Stocked with wooden barrels of rum and empty barrels. Windows several feet from the ground.

Griffith runs to the warehouse, hurriedly unlocks the bolts across the door and enters. He locks it from the inside and SIGHS in relief.

Mary looks up and sees a raging battle. Laborers are beaten and shot. Soldiers are attacked with rocks and sticks.

Clutching Papi's earring, Mary gently places his head on the ground, stands and looks around.

Mary spots Griffith entering the warehouse. She gives the earring a tight squeeze, opens her fist and determinedly puts the earring in her ear.

She looks down at the tear in her dress, RIPS off a strip of material and purposefully looks around. She walks a few yards away, picks up a stick, wraps the material around it and strides over to Martha's beignet stand. She dips the stick in a bottle of kerosene and lights it on the coal pot.

Mary rushes over to the warehouse, brandishing the torch and the bottle of kerosene.

Griffith stands on a barrel and looks out the dirty glass window. He sees Mary approaching. He jumps off the barrel and frantically looks around the room.

Mary tosses the kerosene onto the building and touches the torch to it. The building quickly catches fire. She throws the torch up to the window and misses. The torch falls to the ground, still lit. Big Man steps forward, picks up the torch and easily tosses it. The torch SMASHES through the window and lands on a wooden rum-filled barrel, a ring of fire forms around the top of it.

           MARY
        Nice job, Big Man!

He smiles and nods his head.

           MARY (CONT'D)
        You like that name?

He smiles bigger and nods his approval.

PART 2

FIREBURN

INT./EXT. WAREHOUSE–DAY

Beads of sweat pour off Griffith's head as he rolls a barrel to a back window. He sees the torch land and works faster. Smoke quickly fills the building. He COUGHS.

Griffith climbs onto the barrel, reaches the window and SHATTERS it. He climbs out and falls to the ground with a THUD. An EXPLOSION is heard in the warehouse.

EXT. FORT FREDERIK–DAY

COMMANDER OF THE FORT
Retreat!

Soldiers retreat on horse and on foot in different directions, some to the fort and others to the street. Laborers remain.

A crowd forms in front of the burning warehouse. Laborers CHEER. EXPLOSIONS in the warehouse sound like cannons.

Axeline joins the crowd and CHANTS.

AXELINE
Fire burn, fire burn, fire burn.

Laborers join in the CHANT. The two words become one loud, thunderous cry: FIREBURN, FIREBURN, FIREBURN!

Several laborers make torches and burn other buildings. Others laborers loot buildings and pull valuables into the street.

Griffith rushes down an alley, mounts a nearby horse and gallops off.

INT. GOVERNOR'S OFFICE–DUSK

The office is elaborate and meticulous.

Governor Garde sits at his desk, casually smoking his pipe. His lieutenant governor, aides and a disheveled, infuriated Griffith stand.

> **GOVERNOR GARDE**
> I will have my commander make an official report of the incident in the morning.

> **GRIFFITH**
> Incident?

> **GOVERNOR GARDE**
> Thank you for your visit, Mr. Griffith.

> **GRIFFITH**
> This is not a social visit, Governor. Lives are at stake!

> **GOVERNOR GARDE**
> I understand. The laborers are angry that things did not go their way and an angry woman burned your warehouse.

> **GRIFFITH**
> I do not believe this!

Griffith heads for the door.

> **GRIFFITH (CONT'D)**
> I am not going to sit around and wait to be slaughtered while you do paperwork.

The lieutenant governor WHISPERS in the governor's ear.

LT. GOVERNOR
This is an election year, sir. This incident could be helpful for your re-election.

The governor considers for a moment and CALLS after Griffith.

GOVERNOR GARDE
Griffith!

Griffith turns and looks at the governor.

GOVERNOR GARDE (CONT'D)
My men will handle this.

GRIFFITH
Whatever happens, Mary Thomas is mine.

Griffith leaves. The governor addresses his aides.

GOVERNOR GARDE
You all are dismissed. Lieutenant, stay.

The aides leave. The governor pours himself a drink.

GOVERNOR GARDE (CONT'D)
What is your take on all this? Do you think any of our men were really killed?

LT. GOVERNOR
I see no reason why he would lie, sir. And, if he is telling the truth, it is an excellent opportunity

for the royal court back in Denmark to hear good reports of your brilliant leadership, rather than the lies your adversaries have been spreading.

GOVERNOR GARDE

Yes, of course. My thoughts exactly.

LT. GOVERNOR

However, sir, if he is lying, a strategic man such as yourself must consider the best way to cease a lying tongue.

GOVERNOR GARDE

Get the commander in here.

LT. GOVERNOR

Yes, sir. And what about Mary Thomas?

GOVERNOR GARDE

Who?

LT. GOVERNOR

The woman who appears to be instigating the trouble, sir.

GOVERNOR GARDE

Oh, yes, yes, of course.

LT. GOVERNOR

Shall we make it a priority to get to her before Mr. Griffith does?

GOVERNOR GARDE

If you would stop your rattling, I would have a chance to tell you my plans.

LT. GOVERNOR

Yes, sir.

GOVERNOR GARDE

Lieutenant.

LT. GOVERNOR

Sir?

GOVERNOR GARDE

Bring me this Mary woman before Griffith gets to her.

LT. GOVERNOR

Brilliant plan, sir. And sir, I am sure your plan includes telling the commander that you are not concerned whether he brings Mary to you dead or alive.

The governor looks absentmindedly through papers on his desk.

GOVERNOR GARDE

Oh yes, yes, Lieutenant. I have notes somewhere around here to that effect.

EXT. FORT FREDERIK–DUSK

Mary looks around at the chaos and goes back and sits next to Papi's body. She holds his hand and mourns.

MARY

Papi, that was for you.

Singer, Susanna and Axeline approach and console her for a while before talking.

SUSANNA

(To Mary)

What now?

Mary stands and looks at Papi.

MARY

It's done.

SUSANNA

Done? It just started.

MARY

Papi can rest in peace now.

SUSANNA

A few buildings burned and you're finished? They'll rebuild them and nothing will change.

MARY

I'm done, Susanna.

A crowd forms and CHANTS. The crowd grows.

CROWD

Mary! Mary! Mary!

SUSANNA

They don't seem to think so.

Cy, Martha and Tilda move to the front of the crowd and join in the CHANT.

SINGER

Revenge is not the way.

MARY

I'm not trying to make a way.

SUSANNA

Mary, you started something tonight and the time is ripe to finish it!

SINGER

It's not just about timing. The spirit has to be right. Revenge spoils everything.

SUSANNA

Maybe that's exactly what we need!

MARY

I don't care what either of you do, I'm done.

SUSANNA

Well then, Papi died for nothing.

Mary looks at Susanna, Papi's body and at the crowd. Cy runs up to Mary and gives her a torch.

Mary looks at Singer defiantly, steps closer to the crowd, and SHOUTS.

MARY
We finish what we start!

Mary raises her torch.

MARY (CONT'D)
Fireburn!

The crowd YELLS triumphantly, torches raised.

CROWD
Fireburn!

EXT. FORT FREDERIK–ALLEY WAY–NIGHT

Smoky area lit by smoldering buildings. Rubble, looted goods and dead bodies litter the street.

Tilda and family sit under a tree. The children eat scraps of food. Tilda's mother tends to the father's leg.

Mary walks with an arm load of clean bandages and gives them to Susanna, Axeline and Martha, along with other women. They bandage the injured.

AXELINE
Mary, what are we going to do with Papi?

SUSANNA
Hush, gal.

MARY
It's okay. We have to think about all of the bodies.

AXELINE
I saw a shovel next to the fort.

SUSANNA
We'll need more shovels.

MARY
Burn them.

The women look at Mary with shocked displeasure.

SUSANNA
It's not proper!

MARY
Neither is killing people.

AXELINE
At least let's bury Papi.

MARY
They all get burned.

Singer approaches Mary and he beckons for her to walk with him.

SINGER
You still vex with me?

MARY
You still here?

SINGER
I guess that means "yes."

MARY
Why are you here? To see me fail?

> **SINGER**
> Fail?

Mary nods her head.

> **SINGER (CONT'D)**
> I didn't say you'd fail. It's all what's in here.

Singer taps his chest.

> **MARY**
> What does that have to do with anything?

> **SINGER**
> Revenge and love are seeds that bear different fruit. One is good, the other is poison.

> **MARY**
> I don't care.

> **SINGER**
> That's my point.

Mary storms off toward—

—THE WATERFRONT

Sandy. A pier looms over the water. Several small fishing boats, turned upside down, line the shore.

Mary plops down on the sand.

RUSTLING NOISE. Mary turns suddenly toward the NOISE and sees nothing. She settles down and picks up stones and skips them into the water. Shuffling NOISE.

MARY
Who's there?

Mary gets up and looks around. She walks toward the closest boat, stoops and lifts it. A large crab scurries away and startles her. She drops the boat. She CHUCKLES and relaxes.

A large hand roughly covers Mary's mouth. She lets out a muffled SCREAM and struggles to free herself. A soldier presses a gun into her side.

SOLDIER
Shut up! If you get me out of this hell hole, you may live to see another day.

The soldier removes his hand from Mary's mouth.

MARY
Go to hell!

He jabs the gun into Mary's side and pulls her head back, WHISPERING menacingly into her ear.

SOLDIER
If I go, you go with me.

Mary turns to face him and spits in his face. The soldier roughly slaps her and Mary falls to the ground. The soldier glares at her and wipes his face. He grabs her feet and drags her to a boat, takes rope off of it and ties Mary's hands in front of her.

As the soldier stands, Mary grabs a fistful of sand and scoots away from him. He lunges for her and she throws the sand into his face. The soldier GROANS loudly in discomfort and quickly stumbles down to the water. He washes his eyes. Mary runs toward the camp, YELLING.

> **MARY**
> Help! Help!

Singer and several men run toward Mary. When Mary is a few yards away from the camp the soldier grabs her, holding her from behind.

> **SOLDIER**
> Tell them to back off or I will shoot your head off. We are going over to that horse.

The soldier motions with his head toward a horse that is tied to a huge tree and points the gun at Mary's head.

> **MARY**
> Don't come closer. Just give him the horse.

> **SOLDIER**
> Everybody get in front, where I can see you!
> (To Cy)
> You, boy! Go untie that horse.

Cy glares at the soldier. Martha nudges him.

Cy stubbornly walks to the horse and slowly unties it.

The soldier cautiously approaches the horse, pulling Mary with him. The soldier looks around while the laborers look on silently.

The soldier and Mary get to the horse. The soldier reaches for the reigns and Cy snatches them away.

CY

Let Mary go!

The soldier backhands Cy's face. Cy falls, pulling the reigns, causing the horse to rear and NEIGH. The startled soldier releases Mary. Cy releases the horse. The horse gallops away.

Lewis jumps out of the tree, attacks and disarms the soldier, kicking the gun aside. Singer grabs the gun and aims it at the soldier. Cy and Martha untie Mary.

Big Man rushes forward and helps Lewis. Jonas comes forward and brutally beats the soldier. Mary stops him.

MARY

That's enough! Tie him up.

Jonas glares at Mary, kicks the soldier and walks away. Big Man ties the soldier's hands and feet.

LEWIS

(to Singer, referring to the gun)

You might want to put that thing away before you hurt yourself.

Singer and Lewis go to Mary.

SINGER/LEWIS

You okay?

Mary nods her head. She is shaken.

Lewis protectively puts his arms around Mary and chastises Singer.

LEWIS
Good thing I came along when I did.

MARY
Where have you been?

LEWIS
(offering his cheek to Mary)
Don't I at least get a "thank you" kiss?
Mary's mood lightens. She ignores his cheek.

MARY
Thank you. Where have you been?

LEWIS
Taking care of business.

SINGER
What business would that be?

LEWIS
Nothing that concerns you.

LEWIS (CONT'D)
So, what's the plan Mary?

AXELINE
We don't have one.

MARY
Yes, we do.

All eyes turn to Mary.

MARY (CONT'D)

From here we move on to the plantations and crushing stations. We burn them and the fields to the ground.

SUSANNA

Now you're talking!

MARY

We make them suffer.

Mary, Susanna and the others talk. Lewis and Singer step away.

LEWIS

I have hated you my entire life, but Fapi is right, blood is thicker than water and we might not make it out of this alive.

Lewis sticks out his hand, for a handshake. Singer ignores Lewis' hand.

SINGER

Just like that? I should suddenly trust you now?

LEWIS

Our mother died, doing whatever she needed to do to give us a roof over our heads. This is what she would want.

Singer reflects for a moment and then sticks his hand out. They shake hands hesitatingly.

SINGER
For her.

**EXT. A SHACK NEAR BURNING CANE FIELDS–
NIGHT**

*Jonas shakes hands with a soldier. The soldier hands him
some papers. They squat and Jonas draws a map.*

INT. GOVERNOR'S OFFICE–NIGHT

*Governor Garde, his lieutenant governor, aides and
commander DISCUSS the situation. They study a map on the
desk.*

*The commander illustrates on the map. The governor smokes
his ever-present pipe and looks on nonchalantly.*

COMMANDER OF THE FORT
The laborers have burned many structures in the
immediate vicinity of Fort Frederik. I anticipate
they will move in an easterly fashion and continue
their attack, perhaps even as far as Christiansted.

GOVERNOR GARDE
All the way to Christiansted? Surely, it will blow
over before it gets to that.

COMMANDER OF THE FORT
I have men reported dead and others missing. We
cannot afford to be caught by surprise.

GOVERNOR GARDE
What do you propose?

COMMANDER OF THE FORT
First, we send a boat to get reinforcement from St. Thomas...

GOVERNOR GARDE
I will not be humiliated by having reinforcement come from St. Thomas!

COMMANDER OF THE FORT
May I remind you that we are outnumbered, sir?

GOVERNOR GARDE
I would rather die than be the laughing stock of the entire royal court back in Denmark!

COMMANDER OF THE FORT
You may have your wish soon enough.

EXT. FORT FREDERIK–NIGHT

Mary uses a stick and draws a map of the island's estates, plantations and sugar cane crushing stations in the dirt. Singer, Susanna and Axeline look on.

MARY
Has anyone seen Lewis?

Mary scans the area quickly, then proceeds. Everyone shakes their head.

MARY (CONT'D)
First we take—

AXELINE
We should take Estate Carlton first!

> **SUSANNA**
> Why?

> **AXELINE**
> Because they have the best cotillions and the planters and their wives will be so mad if we burn it!

Susanna looks at her in disbelief and Singer stifles a LAUGH.

> **MARY**
> We burn the sugar cane fields, estates and crushing stations.

> **AXELINE**
> Why?

> **MARY**
> That's how they make money.

> **AXELINE**
> Oh, that's a good idea too.

> **MARY**
> For now, we rest. Tomorrow will be a long day!

EXT. FORT FREDERIK–FOLLOWING DAY

About one third of laborers from the previous day are present. Several laborers rummage through the food stands and debris, eating what they find.

Mary, Singer, Susanna and Axeline move throughout the area and enlist help. They meet up again, each with 10-20 laborers.

AXELINE

Where did everybody disappear to?

SINGER

Probably back at the plantations.

AXELINE

Maybe we should too.

SUSANNA

We can't turn back now.

MARY

We have to. Look around, Susanna! We need an army. We cannot do it.

SUSANNA

If we stick together we can do it.

MARY

We need more than a handful of hungry laborers.

She takes deep breaths and looks at the sky.

MARY (CONT'D)

Buddhoe, Papi – what must we do now?

GALLOPING horse. Soldier with raised white flag, slows to a trot and stops. SHOUTS. Laborers stay a safe distance away and look on inquisitively as the soldier YELLS.

SOLDIER WITH FLAG

Mary Thomas! Is there a Mary Thomas here?

Mary moves forward. Singer grabs her arm, pulling her and TALKING softly.

SINGER
This is not good.

Mary snatches her arm away.

SINGER (CONT'D)
(to the soldier)
What do you want with her?

SOLDIER WITH FLAG
By order of Governor Janus August Garde, all laborers are ordered to return to their plantations at once. Any laborers refusing to do so will be presumed rebels and executed. All will be forgotten if Mary Thomas surrenders now.

Mary slowly approaches the soldier as he raises his gun.

MARY
The governor's plan for victory is to have a single woman surrender!

The soldier gets off of his horse and takes rope from a pouch on his saddle.

SOLDIER WITH FLAG
Mary Thomas?

MARY
Yes. I am Mary Thomas.

The soldier reaches for Mary's hands and ties the rope around them.

Susanna approaches.

> **SUSANNA**
> Wait! I'm Mary Thomas.

> **SOLDIER WITH FLAG**
> Then why did she say she was Mary Thomas?

> **SUSANNA**
> She was trying to protect me.

Axeline catches on and approaches.

> **AXELINE**
> I'm Mary Thomas.

Several women step forward DECLARING individually.

> **WOMAN 1**
> I'm Mary Thomas.

> **WOMAN 2**
> I'm Mary Thomas.

> **WOMAN 3**
> I'm Mary Thomas.

The soldier watches in anger, snatches the rope from Mary's hands and mounts his horse.

> **SOLDIER WITH FLAG**
> This will not end well for any of you!

The soldier GALLOPS off. Some of the women run after him for several feet, still yelling "I AM MARY THOMAS." Those around Mary celebrate the momentary victory. Jonas approaches Mary, CLAPPING insincerely.

> **JONAS**
> That's so beautiful. But why do you get to make the rules? You're asking advice from dead men and can't even decide what to do with a man who almost killed you.

Singer threatens Jonas with his gun.

> **SINGER**
> Step away from her.

Jonas mockingly cowers in fear.

> **JONAS**
> Yes, manja. Please don't shoot me, manja.

Jonas stands tall and insolent.

> **JONAS (CONT'D)**
> Go ahead and shoot, but your woman is still a coward.

Jonas faces Mary and motions to the tied soldier who had held Mary hostage.

> **JONAS (CONT'D)**
> What are you going to do with him?

The crowd waits expectantly.

Mary looks at the pile of dead bodies on the grand stand.

MARY
He will join the others.

Big Man carries the soldier to the pile of dead bodies and throws the struggling soldier onto it. The soldier glares at Mary.

SOLDIER
I'll see you in hell.

Big Man pours kerosene over the bodies and lights the pile on fire. The soldier SCREAMS in agony.

Mary grabs the gun from Singer's hand, walks briskly to the grand stand and SHOOTS the soldier in the head. She gives the gun to Singer. Laborers watch the bodies burn. Jonas sneers at Mary as she walks away.

EXT. ESTATE GLYNN–DAY

A beautiful plantation stands in the distance. No signs of movement on the expansive grounds and surrounding sugar cane fields.

Mary, Singer, Susanna, Axeline and laborers approach. Mary gives orders.

MARY
Check the shed for horses and weapons and anything we can eat.

Several of the laborers run into the shed and ransack it. They return with machetes, hoes and pickaxes. Another carries a jug of kerosene.

> **MARY (CONT'D)**
> Burn everything!

The laborer with the kerosene pours it around the shed. One group charges the plantation, breaking windows and throwing torches inside. A second group sets fire to the fields. The shed goes up in flames. The laborers watch and CHEER.

Mary, Singer, Susanna, Axeline and the laborers tirelessly burn many plantations, fields and crushing stations, some being, Campo Rico and Catherine's Rest.

EXT. DIRT ROAD–DAY

Smoke fills the air from burning sugar cane fields.

Mary, Singer, Susanna and Axeline move energetically along. The laborers follow along purposefully.

Mary YELLS to the laborers.

> **MARY**
> Estate Barren Spot is ahead. You know what to do!

The laborers attack the plantation with torches and weapons. YELLS of agony and EXPLOSIONS are heard.

> **SUSANNA**
> That's not good.

EXT. ESTATE BARREN'S SPOT–DAY

Mary, Singer, Axeline, Susanna and the remaining laborers run to the plantation. Several laborers are blown up as they charge in the field.

MARY

Come back! Everybody, come back! Something is wrong.

Laborers retreat. In stunned silence, they look at the dead, mutilated bodies. Susanna makes the sign of the cross on her head and chest.

MARY (CONT'D)

They knew we were coming. How?

SUSANNA

It doesn't matter, we can't stop now.

SINGER

Sometimes you have to know when enough is enough.

MARY

We need to hurt them like they hurt us! We need them to know that whoever has betrayed us, did not stop us!

AXELINE

How?

Mary thinks for a few seconds.

MARY

We go to Christiansted and burn all the way to Bassin jailhouse and let the prisoners go!

EXT. DIRT ROAD–DUSK

Mary, Susanna, Axeline and Singer walk slowly. Following them are able-bodied laborers assisting the injured.

An injured laborer keels over. An able-bodied laborer helps him up. Mary glances at them and gives ORDERS.

> **MARY**
> Keep moving everybody. Next stop is Estate Griffith. You can get a good rest there since Griffith is dead.

EXT./INT. ESTATE GRIFFITH–NIGHT

Deserted.

Mary, Susanna, Axeline and Singer near the stables. Singer rushes over, peers inside and REPORTS.

> **SINGER**
> Everything is here. We even have horses.

> **AXELINE**
> And something else!

> **SUSANNA**
> What?

> **AXELINE**
> You'll see.

Able-bodied laborers set up camp.

Mary, Susanna, Axeline and Singer enter—

—ESTATE GRIFFITH

> **AXELINE (CONT'D)**
> Come.

Axeline takes Singer's arm and guides him, Mary and Susanna through the house to—

—GRIFFITH'S STUDY

Axeline opens the door and they enter. Axeline walks over to a bookcase and pulls on several books.

> **AXELINE (CONT'D)**
> Watch this.

Nothing happens as Axeline pulls on several books.

> **SUSANNA**
> We don't have time for your games, Axeline. The kitchen is calling.

Axeline pulls a book and a door knob is revealed. She twists it and the bookcase opens, revealing a room with guns and ammunition. Mary, Singer and Susanna stand in awe of Griffith's gun collection

Singer eagerly inspects the guns. Axeline beams at Singer.

> **AXELINE**
> Tilda told me about it.

> **SUSANNA**
> Good! Now come do some work in the kitchen.

MARY

I'll look for other supplies.

Mary, Susanna, and Alexine leave Singer with the weapons.

Singer is alone. He loads a revolver, aims at the wall, pretends to shoot. He puts the gun into his pants waist. Singer slides the secret panel closed and leaves.

—MASTER BEDROOM

Dimly lit by lantern. Four poster bed, dresser with toiletries and perfumes, large arm chair, vanity with a ceramic pitcher, basin, washcloth and soap. A spacious wooden armoire stands against the opposite wall.

Mary slowly opens the bedroom door, peers inside. She heads to the armoire, opens the double doors and trails her hand over several dresses. Mary studies them and chooses a simple, long-sleeved, white cotton dress.

Mary steps over to the vanity, looks inside the pitcher and pours the water into the basin. She uses the soap and washcloth and wipes herself clean.

Mary slips into the white dress and struggles with the hooks in the back.

SINGER

Let me help you with that.

Mary jumps in surprise and turns to see Singer leaning against the bedroom door.

MARY

How long have you been there?

Singer saunters over to her and slowly hooks her dress.

SINGER
Don't worry, not long enough.

Singer finishes the last hook and goes to the bed and reclines. He admires Mary as she stands facing him.

SINGER (CONT'D)
So, how are we going to do it?

MARY
Do it? Are you out of your mind?

SINGER
Take Government House. How are we going to do it?

Singer looks at her with a boyish grin.

MARY
Oh.

SINGER
What did you think I meant?

MARY
Nothing.

Singer gives her a warm smile, sits up and pats the side of the bed next to him.

SINGER
Come.

Mary looks around the room.

MARY
I need to get oil for the lantern.

SINGER
The lantern can wait.

Mary hesitates, then sits on the edge of the bed. Singer tenderly stares at her.

MARY
Bassin jail house. We...we will...

Singer gently touches Mary's face.

SINGER
I'm listening.

MARY
We'll take them by surprise.

Singer leans in to kiss Mary and she moves closer, her eyes closed. The bedroom door CREAKS. Susanna enters.

Mary springs from the bed. Singer remains calmly seated.

SUSANNA
Sorry!

MARY
No, no, it's okay. I was just coming to look for you.

SUSANNA
It didn't look that way to me!

SINGER
Mary was just filling me in on the plans for Government House.

Susanna gives a knowing smile and turns to leave, while speaking.

SUSANNA
Well, I'll just let you two continue your little planning meeting and you can fill the rest of us in after you're done.

SINGER
Okay.

MARY
No! I was just leaving.

Mary hastily leaves with Susanna. Singer falls back on the bed, SIGHING in frustration. Susanna and Mary walk down the-

—HALLWAY

SUSANNA
Finally, the dog can wag his tail.

MARY
There's no dog wagging any tail here. Nothing happened!

SUSANNA
If you say so.

MARY
I don't even fancy him.

SUSANNA
Just because one dog bites you, doesn't mean all dogs bite.

MARY
I wish you and your tail-wagging, dog-biting self would mind your own business.

Mary gently shoves Susanna and smiles. Susanna CHUCKLES.

EXT. ESTATE GRIFFITH

A campfire lights the yard.

Laborers feast, drink and dance. A scratch band performs. Axeline dances and male laborers take turns dancing with her.

Mary and Susanna exit the house.

Laborers grab Mary and Susanna to dance. They dance next to Axeline. Axeline admires Mary's new outfit.

AXELINE
That's just what I need.

MARY
There's plenty to choose from.

Axeline rushes into Estate Griffith.

—MASTER BEDROOM

Very dimly lit by light from fading lantern.

Axeline enters, spots the armoire, heads for it and opens it. She pulls an armful of dresses out and dumps them on the chair. She presses a red evening gown against her body and dances with it.

SNORING. Startled, Axeline turns and notices Singer asleep in bed. She tosses the red dress on the arm chair. Her own dress drops to the floor.

Quietly, a smiling Axeline snuggles under the covers next to Singer.

EXT. ESTATE GRIFFITH

Mary sits on the ground and eats food. Susanna plops down next to her, takes some food from Mary's plate and eats it.

> **MARY**
> Are you here to tell me about more dogs?

> **SUSANNA**
> No. I'm minding my own business.

> **MARY**
> Good! It just shows you can teach an old dog new tricks.

They LAUGH.

> **SUSANNA**
> Singer must be starving by now.

Susanna grabs Mary's plate and eats.

> **SUSANNA (CONT'D)**
> Too bad I'm busy, or I'd get him some food.

> **MARY**
> He's a grown man, he can get his own food.

> **SUSANNA**
> You mean to tell me you don't care if your soldiers die of starvation and you've filled your belly?

Mary hesitates for a moment.

> **MARY**
> Just when I thought you really were learning to mind your own business.

Susanna shrugs, feigning innocence.

Mary heads toward Estate Griffith holding a plate heaped with food.

—MASTER BEDROOM

Axeline leans on her elbow, staring at Singer and lightly traces his face with her finger. Eyes still closed, Singer slowly rouses and gives an appreciative smile. He reaches for her hand and kisses it.

> **SINGER**
> Dreams do come true.

Mary, smiling, enters with the plate of food. She GASPS at the site. Singer opens his eyes and does a double take at Axeline and Mary.

Axeline casually reclines on her elbow.

Singer, fully clothed, springs from the bed and rushes toward Mary. She backs away from him.

MARY
You bastard!

Mary flings the plate of food at him. Singer dodges the plate.

SINGER
It's not what it looked like!

MARY
You think I'm stupid?

SINGER
I thought it was you.

AXELINE
We don't look alike.

Mary storms out the door and runs down the hall. Singer rushes after her.

SINGER
Mary, wait!

Mary does not stop.

—GROUNDS

Mary runs out and Singer pursues. Big Man steps in front of Singer and blocks Singer's path every time Singer tries to move.

> **SINGER (CONT'D)**
> Move!

Big Man picks Singer up by the throat with one hand and wags his finger "no" with the other hand. He puts Singer down.

Singer rubs his throat and YELLS.

> **SINGER (CONT'D)**
> Mary, wait! I can explain!

Mary continues running.

INT. MARY'S SHACK–NIGHT

Mary pushes the door open and storms in. She throws herself onto Papi's bed, hugs a pillow and fights back tears.

EXT. ESTATE GRIFFITH–GROUNDS–NIGHT

The festivities continue. Singer and Big Man sit on the ground. Big Man takes a swig of rum from a bottle and offers it to Singer. Singer refuses. Big Man insists. Singer takes a reluctant sip and hands the bottle back.

The evening progresses, the camp fire has diminished to small flames. Many of the laborers are rowdy and drunk.

Empty bottles lie scattered around Singer and Big Man who are seated and leaning against a tree, arms around each other. Singer turns a bottle upside down, nothing comes out. He throws it to the ground.

Later that evening. The campfire is now glowing coals. Laborers' sleeping bodies dot the grounds.

Susanna walks out of Estate Griffith and onto the porch and spots Axeline brooding on the stairs.

SUSANNA
Where's Mary?

Axeline sadly looks over at Singer and points.

AXELINE
Ask him.

SUSANNA
You alright?

AXELINE
Yea, just dying of a broken heart.

SUSANNA
I thought you were getting a new frock. That will put you in a good mood.

Axeline SIGHS and stands.

AXELINE
Maybe you're right.

Axeline despondently enters Estate Griffith and goes to the—

—MASTER BEDROOM

Axeline stares at the dresses on the chair, walks over to them and chooses the red evening gown from among them. She slowly dons it. She turns and sees her reflection in the mirror and smiles. She struts around the room as though she is a snobby lady, nose in the air. She curtsies and INTRODUCES herself.

AXELINE (CONT'D)
Lady Axeline, thank you.

—GROUNDS

Susanna approaches Singer.

SUSANNA
Where's Mary?

SINGER
Don't know.

SUSANNA
But, you two were...

SINGER
She ran.

SUSANNA
That's one hard-headed woman!

SNORING. Singer falls over. Susanna glances at Singer.

SUSANNA (CONT'D)
Singer? Forget it. I know where she is.

Susanna leaves.

—PERIMETER ROAD

Susanna briskly makes her way down the road.

Men LAUGHING and horses TROTTING. Susanna ducks behind the bush. Griffith, along with a band of armed men, head in the direction of his house. The loyal, but not too smart brothers, Will and Jack head the band.

The men share a flask of rum. Griffith has his own.

> **GRIFFITH**
> "Wait" he says. Wait for reinforcement! I will not wait to be rescued like some helpless woman. We'll fight like men!

The men CHEER.

> **WILL**
> Yes, sir!

> **JACK**
> How will we find them?

Griffith SNIFFS the air.

> **GRIFFITH**
> Sniff the air and follow their stench.

Susanna freezes. Jack SNIFFS the air.

> **JACK**
> I smell roasted pork.

Susanna runs once she is no longer able to see them.

Griffith stops his horse when the shadow of his house comes into view. He motions for the men to stop and pulls out a pair of binoculars from a pouch on his saddle. He peers through them.

GRIFFITH
Well, well, well…

Griffith hands the binoculars to Jack who looks through them and LAUGHS as he hands the binoculars to Will.

WILL
This is going to be too easy.

GRIFFITH
It is time for justice!

Griffith digs his heels into his horse. It GALLOPS at full speed. The men follow.

INT. MARY'S SHACK—NIGHT

Mary is asleep. Susanna bursts in, out of breath.

SUSANNA
Griffith! He's here!

Mary jumps up.

MARY
What?

SUSANNA
Griffith is here!

MARY
That's nonsense, Susanna! He's dead.

SUSANNA

I don't know how, but Griffith is alive and he has men with guns!

PART 3

JUDGEMENT

1760

EXT./INT. ESTATE GRIFFITH—NIGHT

Griffith and his men swoop in and catch the sleeping laborers off guard. He YELLS his command.

GRIFFITH

Shoot anything that moves!

GUNSHOTS ring out and laborers SCREAM in pain.

—MASTER BEDROOM

Axeline runs to the bedroom window and peers out at the bloody scene.

—GROUNDS

Laborers stagger for shelter. Many run to the surrounding fields. The remaining laborers aren't able to defend themselves. A massacre ensues.

Mary and Susanna, hidden in the sugar cane field, take in the sight.

Singer and Big Man run. Griffith spots Singer and points to him. Griffith directs a group of armed men, and then Will and Jack.

GRIFFITH

I want that one alive.

You two, secure the house.

Will and Jack cautiously enter—

Angela Golden Bryan

—ESTATE GRIFFITH

Guns poised, Will and Jack creep down the hall and inspect each room carefully.

—MASTER BEDROOM

Axeline exits the bedroom and enters the hallway. FOOTSTEPS. She runs back into the bedroom and softly closes the door. She bumps against the dresser and a perfume bottle falls and SHATTERS.

—HALLWAY

Will and Jack look toward the master bedroom. Jack WHISPERS and motions toward the master bedroom.

> **JACK**
> I think it came from there.

Will points to a different room down the hall.

> **WILL**
> I'll check that one.

> **JACK**
> Coward.

—MASTER BEDROOM

Jack slowly turns the door knob. Axeline jumps into the armoire and quietly closes the door. A small piece of her dress catches in the door.

Jack enters and SNIFFS the air. He looks around and studies the room. He goes over to the bed and looks under it.

JACK (CONT'D)
Come out, come out, wherever you are.

Jack goes to the armoire and opens the door. Axeline stiffens in fear. He sweeps through the dresses with his hand as Axeline lies on the floor of the armoire, covered by the dresses' hems. He closes the armoire and walks to the bedroom door.

Ready to exit and hand on door knob, he studies the room again and notices the red piece of material caught in the armoire door. He walks and jerks the armoire open and holds onto the piece of material, pulling it. He lifts the dresses and exposes Axeline.

JACK (CONT'D)
Ah hah!

He pulls Axeline out of the armoire.

JACK (CONT'D)
This is my lucky day.

Jack pins Axeline against the wall and gropes her. She struggles. Axeline grabs a perfume bottle, from the dresser, and smashes it against his temple. His temple bleeds as he rubs his eyes and SCREAMS in pain.

JACK (CONT'D)
Agh!

Will YELLS from the hallway.

> **WILL**
> You okay?

RUNNING down the hallway.

Jack rubs his eyes. Axeline grabs the porcelain pitcher from the vanity and breaks it over his head. He falls to the floor and lies motionless. Axeline runs to the curtained window, opens it, examines the distance dubiously. She runs back to the armoire and hides in it again, quietly shutting the door, this time making sure that her dress is inside the armoire.

Will KICKS the door open and stands in the doorway, gun raised and cocked. He surveys the room, spots Jack and puts away his gun when he sees the opened window.

Will runs to Jack and shakes him.

Will gets the basin of water and pours it over Jack's face. Jack SPUTTERS.

—GROUNDS

Will and Jack approach Griffith who is a few yards away. Jack is wet and his temple bruised. He explains the situation to Will.

> **JACK**
> She, I mean, he was huge...had a machete at my throat...

> **WILL**
> Is that when he poured the perfume on you?

JACK

Yes! I mean, No! He hit me hard and I fell and the perfume spilt all over me.

Griffith turns and sees them.

GRIFFITH

All secure?

WILL

All secure, sir.

GRIFFITH

(to Jack)

So secure that you had time for a bath and some of my wife's perfume?

JACK

I...

Griffith holds up his hand and shakes his head "No".

Other armed men bring Singer to Griffith. They throw him at Griffith's feet, he is bound with rope. An armed man hands Griffith the gun that Singer had on him. Griffith inspects the gun as he SPEAKS.

GRIFFITH

You have good taste, Singer. This is highly collectable. They stopped making these five years ago.

Griffith puts the gun in his waist.

GRIFFITH (CONT'D)
I expected more from you, Singer.

WILL
Whether they're high yellow or black as the night, you can't trust any of them, sir.

GRIFFITH
Where is Mary, Singer?

Singer remains silent.

GRIFFITH (CONT'D)
Okay, we'll play it your way. Men...have some fun with him for a while, keep him alive.

Griffith heads to his house.

INT./EXT. ESTATE GRIFFITH-NIGHT

Axeline cautiously opens the bedroom door and creeps down the hall. She hastens to the front door, reaching for the knob.

Griffith climbs the stairs of the porch and puts his hand on the door knob. He pulls the door open just as Axeline places her hand on the knob.

Axeline jumps and hides behind the drapes.

Griffith enters the foyer and looks around. He strolls into his study and lights a lantern.

Axeline eases her way from behind the drapes and quietly goes out the front door. She rushes off the porch and onto the unlit grounds. She stumbles on a dead body and CRIES out.

Will and Jack spin around and peer into the darkness.

JACK
What was that?

WILL
Maybe it's that big, strong buck, coming to put more perfume on you.

Will assumes a zombie-like stance and makes a ghoulish MOAN, pretending to attack Jack.

JACK
Cut it out, that's not funny!

A cat runs out from behind a tree. Jack jumps. Will LAUGHS.

WILL
Agh!!! The kitty cat is going to get you.

Axeline spots the armed men and Singer.

Will LAUGHS uncontrollably. Jack kicks Singer several times before tying him to a post.

Will stops LAUGHING and pushes Jack aside.

WILL (CONT'D)
Move over and let me show you how it's done.

Will beats Singer, while QUESTIONING him.

WILL (CONT'D)
Where's Mary?

Singer stifles CRIES of pain.

WILL (CONT'D)
Where is she?

SINGER
I don't know!

JACK
So you do speak.

Jack punches Singer in the face. Singer is bloody and eyes swollen, barely conscious.

Griffith returns.

GRIFFITH
Cut him down.

They cut Singer from the post and his body collapses to the ground with a soft THUD. The sound of his body hitting the ground covers the noise of Mary and Susanna's footsteps outside of the stable.

Griffith takes his gun from his waist, appears to aim at Singer and FIRES. Singer is startled, then slumps in motionless relief, eyes shut. The armed men LAUGH loudly.

Mary stifles a CRY as she looks at Singer's limp body. Susanna takes Mary's arm and gently pulls her to leave.

SUSANNA
There's nothing we can do.

Mary leaves as Susanna comforts her.

GRIFFITH
Next time I won't miss, boy.

(*To the armed men*)

Take him inside the stables. Keep a good eye on him.

From her viewing area, Axeline watches as the armed men drag Singer to the—

—STABLE

Will and Jack tie Singer up and stand guard by the door.

Axeline silently moves toward the back of the stable. She peers into a window and spots Singer.

EXT. DIRT ROAD–NIGHT

Tall, thick foliage lines either side of the road. Mary and Susanna trudge along.

> **SUSANNA**
> It's not your fault.

MOVEMENT in the bushes. Mary and Susanna stop and look around. They see nothing.

> **MARY**
> If I hadn't taken everyone to Estate Griffith, Singer and everyone else would still be alive.

> **SUSANNA**
> You couldn't know that Griffith was still alive.

RUSTLING of bushes. Mary and Susanna jerk around and examine the bushes.

> **MARY**
> Come out whoever it is or I will shoot.

Mary puts her hand on her waist on an imaginary gun. Susanna looks at Mary's empty waist.

SUSANNA
Yes, and I'll chop you to pieces with my machete.

Mary looks at Susanna's empty hands. Axeline bounces out of the bushes.

AXELINE
You're alive!

SUSANNA
I didn't think I'd ever see you again.

Axeline looks at Mary apologetically and touches her arm.

AXELINE
I'm sorry about Singer. I didn't know you two...

MARY
...It's okay, he wasn't interested in me.

AXELINE
You joking? He was asleep the whole time. When he realized it was me and not you, he almost died.

Susanna gives Mary an "I told you so" look.

AXELINE
His heart belongs to you.

MARY
Belonged...

AXELINE
It still does.

MARY
He's dead.

AXELINE
No, I saw him.

Susanna grabs Axeline by the shoulders and shakes her.

SUSANNA
Are you sure?

AXELINE
I promise you.

Susanna releases her and rubs her head pensively. Mary turns in the direction that they came from and picks up the pace.

SUSANNA
Slow down, gal.

MARY
We've got to go back!

Susanna and Axeline follow. Susanna grabs Mary's arm. Mary pulls free of Susanna's grasp.

MARY (CONT'D)
We have to help.

SUSANNA
Mary, stop right now!

Mary stops and faces Susanna.

> **SUSANNA (CONT'D)**
> Yes, he needs our help. But what can we do against all of those men?

> **MARY**
> I could turn myself in.

> **SUSANNA**
> Then he'd kill you and Singer. That won't solve anything.

SHUFFLING of feet. Mary, Susanna and Axeline take cover in the bushes.

A weary woman with five children in tow. A sleeping toddler is tied to her back. A young child carries an infant. Two smaller children drag their feet.

> **YOUNG CHILD**
> Mommy, I can't carry him anymore.

> **WEARY WOMAN**
> We're almost at Anna's Hope.

> **YOUNG CHILD**
> You said that a long time ago.

> **WEARY WOMAN**
> Hush, child. We have to keep moving.

Mary, Susanna and Axeline step into the road. The weary woman freezes in her tracks. The young child looks on curiously. The two smaller children hide behind their mother's skirt.

MARY

Good evening, Miss. We are not here for trouble.

The weary woman nods a cautious greeting.

MARY (CONT'D)

What's happening at Anna's Hope?

WEARY WOMAN

People are meeting there, then going to the country. It's the only safe place.

Susanna pulls a Johnnycake from her pocket and breaks it into pieces. The children look on hungrily. She gives a piece to the young child. The two younger children flock to her as she extends her hand. Susanna takes the infant from the young child and cradles it.

The mother appears relieved.

MARY

We'll get you there.

Susanna and Axeline look at her questioningly.

WEARY WOMAN

Thank you, Miss.

They walk down the road. Susanna pulls Mary aside.

SUSANNA

What are you doing? We need to be about our business.

MARY
Anna's Hope could be our only hope to get help.

EXT. ESTATE ANNA'S HOPE–GROUNDS–NIGHT

A rustic stone gate surrounds the manicured grounds. Trees dot the property and a large, vacant windmill stands majestically in the foreground. A medium sized stone house is several yards away.

Tilda, her mother, father, brother and sister, along with Martha, Cy and a few other laborers sit as a group. There are other small groups scattered throughout the grounds, many consisting of families with children.

A large campfire is in the center. Several laborers sit around. CHATTER.

COMMOTION. Several laborers rush to the gate. They assist several badly injured laborers and take them to the campfire. They are given water and their wounds are tended to. Jonas looks on.

Many laborers from the various groups surround the new arrivals. MURMUR. Cy joins the crowd. Martha approaches and stays on the periphery.

JONAS
Looks like you all saw some action.

INJURED LABORER 1
She told us that Estate Griffith would be empty...

JONAS
She?

INJURED LABORER 1

Mary Thomas.

JONAS

She's going to get everybody killed.

(Pause)

Where is she now?

INJURED LABORER 1

Somebody said they saw her running from the estate long before the action started.

JONAS

Almost like she knew they were coming. I wonder how much they paid her.

CY

You're a stupid man if you think Mary would do that!

Martha pushes through the crowd and confronts Jonas.

MARTHA

I should correct my son for disrespecting an adult. But you don't deserve respect. You don't know her like we do.

JONAS

I know her well enough.

Martha takes Cy's arm and walks away with him. She takes Cy behind a tree and grabs his ear and twists it.

CY
Ow! Why did you do that?

MARTHA
If I ever hear you call an adult "stupid" again I will beat you so hard you won't be able to sit for a week.

CY
But you said it was okay!

Martha gives his ear another twist. Cy flinches.

Back at the campfire Jonas holds the attention of those nearby. More laborers from various groups approach.

JONAS
Now you see what happens when you follow weak people. Come, fight with me!

Mary, Susanna, Axeline, the weary woman and her children arrive at the gate. Cy strains to see the new arrivals. He runs and meets them.

CY
I knew you'd come!

Cy escorts Mary, Susanna and Axeline to Martha, Tilda and her family.

CY (CONT'D)
Mary, there's a man saying bad things about you.

SUSANNA
What did he say?

MARY

It doesn't matter.

CY

He's telling people that the manja paid you to leave
everybody at Estate Griffith to be killed.

Mary's face tightens.

SUSANNA

That's a lie from the pits of hell! Who's this liar?

MARTHA

Over there.

*Mary looks over at Jonas. As he ADDRESSES the crowd they
APPLAUD.*

Mary steps closer.

JONAS

I don't need clapping. I need serious people who
are ready to fight. Where was your Mary Thomas
when most of you got slaughtered?

*A laborer looks in Mary's direction and nudges a fellow
laborer. Several laborers turn. MURMURING.*

Mary SHOUTS.

MARY

You want to ask me something?

Everyone in the crowd looks back at Mary. MURMURING.

JONAS

(To Mary)

What a surprise to see you here, and looking so well.

MARY

What's your problem with me? We all want the same thing.

JONAS

Tell us, how did you manage to save yourself while so many people were killed?

SUSANNA

She doesn't have to answer the likes of you! Did you question everybody else?

JONAS

Everybody else wasn't giving orders and pretending to be the manja.

SUSANNA

She's better than...

JONAS

Men died while she was...where? Nobody knows. Mary, what were you doing while everyone died?

MARY

She's right, I don't have to answer to you.

Mary turns and walks away. Susanna follows. Mary motions for Susanna to leave her alone. Cy, Martha, Axeline and Tilda look on helplessly.

MURMURING from people in the crowd. Many give Mary disapproving glares.

Mary goes out of sight to the small—

—WINDMILL

Neatly kept graveyard for rusted tools and miscellaneous items. A broken wheelbarrow, a rustic table, along with wooden chairs with legs missing line the wall, along with several bales of hay. The center is clear.

Mary sits inside and rests against a bale of hay. She stares blankly at the wall.

The crowd continues to listen to Jonas' passionate discourse. Many nod their heads in agreement and CLAP wildly.

Injured Laborer 1 approaches Susanna and motions for her to follow him.

He uses a cane, fashioned from a thick branch, to support himself. They walk away from the crowd and come within hearing distance of the windmill.

Mary springs to her feet. She edges closer to the door, peeks outside and then cocks her ear to the entrance.

> **INJURED LABORER 1**
> We need to join up with Jonas. He's a strong leader and if we want to make a difference we have to stick together.

> **SUSANNA**
> What you do is none of my business.

> **INJURED LABORER 1**
> Listen.

SUSANNA
I'm listening.

INJURED LABORER 1
We need everybody. It doesn't make sense having one group here and one group there.

SUSANNA
It doesn't matter as long as we are all fighting for the same thing.

INJURED LABORER 1
What's Mary fighting for?

Susanna is silent. Injured Laborer 1 walks away. Susanna is pensive as she walks back toward the crowd.

Mary stares out the door as Susanna walks back to the crowd.

INT. ESTATE GRIFFITH—STABLE—NIGHT

Horses are in their stalls. Bales of hay line the walls. A wooden work table with chairs takes center stage. A small wooden chest rests on the table.

Singer lies on the floor, bound with rope.

Will opens the chest. It contains knives and a sharpening stone. He selects a knife and sharpens it deliberately.

Jack throws a bucket of water onto Singer's face. Singer rouses and attempts to wipe his face. His hands are bound.

JACK
Nap time is over!

Griffith enters.

GRIFFITH

Everything ready?

WILL

Yes, sir.

Will takes a flask from his shirt pocket, bites off the cork and empties it into his mouth.

GRIFFITH

Not too much, you'll need steady hands.

WILL

No chance of me having too much, sir. The Darkies drank every ounce of rum on the plantation.

GRIFFITH

I still have my stash.

JACK

No, sir. That's gone too.

GRIFFITH

And just how would you know that?

JACK

I...we, checked to make sure it was still there because we knew you'd like some for later, sir.

GRIFFITH

Glad you have my best interests at heart.

JACK
Yes, sir!

GRIFFITH
Take a break for now.

Will and Jack leave.

Griffith goes over to the horses and slowly examines one of them. Running his hands over it admiringly.

Griffith reclines on the chair, feet crossed on the table. He lights a cigar and savors it as he TALKS.

GRIFFITH (CONT'D)
Horses are such beautiful creatures...yet practical. They work hard, you breed them and you just keep getting your investment back. Now you would not want all of them breeding of course, because you might spread some bad genetic qualities. That's where castration comes in. Niggers are just like horses, Singer.

Griffith picks up a knife and examines its edge.

GRIFFITH (CONT'D)
I could have killed you...but your mamma was a pretty special woman...and with my blood running through your veins, I figured, I won't kill you. But you do need to be disciplined.

SINGER

(hoarse, barely able to speak)
You're not my father!

Griffith gets up and goes over to Singer.

GRIFFITH
Come now, boy, you know better. All the special treatment I've given you over the years. I must say, you and I have similar taste in women. That Mary Thomas, she is feisty, just like your mother. She spoke her mind, even after I would knock the hell out of her.

A seething Singer struggles to get up, Griffith kicks him back down. Griffith pulls a flask from his inner vest pocket and opens it.

GRIFFITH (CONT'D)
Open up. You are going to need this.

Singer does not open his mouth. Griffith bends over and pries Singer's mouth open. Just as Griffith pours the rum, Singer jerks his face from Griffith's grip and turns to the side, causing rum to spill on the side of his face.

GRIFFITH (CONT'D)
Suit yourself.

Griffith exits the stables and addresses Will and Jack.

GRIFFITH (CONT'D)
Round up the rest of the fellows. Let him sit and think about the error of his ways. We have something else to tend to first.

EXT. ESTATE ANNA'S HOPE—GROUNDS—NIGHT

The laborers settle down for the evening. Susanna, Axeline, Cy, Martha, Tilda and her family form a group and lie down on the grass. CHATTER from neighboring groups. An infant CRIES.

    CY
It's too loud here.

Mary spots Cy approaching and hurriedly climbs through the window. She leans against the wall and slumps to the ground.

Cy enters the windmill and inspects it. He kneels next to a bale of hay, bows his head and places his hands in prayer position.

Mary listens.

    CY (CONT'D)
Dear Jesus, thank you for protecting us all and please make the man at the sugar factory give me a job. Amen!

Cy lies down and uses his hands as a pillow.

Mary has an "aha" moment. With a renewed purpose she walks toward the groups.

Jonas takes head counts amongst the various groups. Laborers raise their hands and he acknowledges them. Jonas approaches Susanna, Axeline, Martha, Tilda and her family and addresses them.

The survivors from the Estate Griffith massacre are in a separate group close by. They move in as Jonas speaks.

JONAS

Country folk or fighters?

SUSANNA

What business is it of yours?

JONAS

That's right, you're one of Mary's gang.

SUSANNA

I don't belong to anybody!

JONAS

That's true since, Mary is nowhere to be found.
She's deserted you, again.

SUSANNA

She has more good in her little finger than you do
in your whole body!

JONAS

Is "good" what we need right now?

SUSANNA

All I know is we don't need you!

JONAS

We leave in the morning. Your choice.

Jonas continues on to another group of laborers.

INJURED LABORER 1

(to Susanna)

I wanted to believe in her too.

INJURED LABORER 2
She left us to die once before, why are you
surprised that she's doing it again?

SUSANNA
It's not like that.

They spot Mary approaching. She hails them.

SUSANNA (CONT'D)
See!

MARY
Alright, I've got a plan.

AXELINE
What's your plan?

MARY
I've figured out a way to rescue Singer.

Injured Laborers 1 and 2 shake their heads in disbelief.

INJURED LABORER 1
Your plan is to rescue one person?

They leave and join Jonas.

MARY
We didn't need them anyway.

They give her doubtful looks.

MARY (CONT'D)
You all want to leave too?

SUSANNA
Mary, maybe he has a point.

MARY
I knew you'd desert me too.

SUSANNA
I'm not...

MARY
I don't need any of you!

Mary turns and leaves angrily.

AXELINE
Wait, Mary!

Susanna touches Axeline's arm.

SUSANNA
Let her go. She just needs to calm down.

EXT. DIRT ROAD—NIGHT

With determination, Mary rushes down the dirt road. CRACKLING noise. Mary turns around with a look of concern and quickly scans the area. She picks up her pace, occasionally looking behind.

The Central Sugar Factory is in the distance.

EXT. CENTRAL SUGAR FACTORY—COURTYARD —NIGHT

A dirty, bruised Himmelman, with arms bound, is surrounded by THREE MENACING LABORERS. One holds a pickaxe, another a torch, while another brandishes a machete and kicks Himmelman.

> **MENACING LABORER 1**
> ...time for you to die!

Mary approaches and quickly assesses the scene.

The machete-wielding Menacing Laborer 1 pins Himmelman to the ground and exposes Himmelman's neck. He raises the machete overhead and prepares to strike.

Mary YELLS.

> **MARY**
> Wait! Stop!

Menacing Laborer 1 stops and they turn their attention to Mary.

> **MARY (CONT'D)**
> This man is not our enemy.

> **MENACING LABORER 1**
> They are all our enemies.

> **MARY**
> He's helping us.

> **MENACING LABORER 1**
> How?

Mary looks at Himmelman.

MARY
He said he'll give us whatever we need, that's why I'm here.

MENACING LABORER 2
Give it to us? We will kill him and take it all!

Menacing Laborer 1 positions his machete to strike.

MARY
Wait!

Menacing Laborer 1 stops. They look at Mary questioningly.

MARY (CONT'D)
When he gave Juju a job, the Obeah woman put a spell of protection on him.

MENACING LABORER 1
Juju?

MARY
Yes, everybody knows he's the Obeah woman's son!

Menacing Laborers 2 and 3 quickly step away from Himmelman. Menacing Laborer 1 hesitatingly turns to them and WHISPERS.

MENACING LABORER 1
You ever hear of Juju?

MENACING LABORER 3

It doesn't matter! The last person who touched someone she protected died a bad, bad death.

A wet spot appears in the front of Menacing Laborer 2's pants as he pees on himself. Menacing Laborer 1 faces Mary.

MENACING LABORER 1

How come I never heard about this before?

MARY

This is a big island, you can't hear everything. Mr. Himmelman, does Juju still work for you?

HIMMELMAN

Uh, Juju moved back to Anguilla. But he loved it here.

Himmelman's voice grows more confident.

HIMMELMAN (CONT'D)

I'm very grateful to the Obeah woman for her protection.

At the mention of the Obeah women's name the laborers shrink in fear. Menacing Laborer 1 appears calm.

MARY

Listen, we're wasting time. There's an army forming in Anna's Hope and they need strong leaders and men like all you.

Menacing Laborer 1 stands tall at the mention of "strong leaders".

—STORAGE SHACK

Dark. Shelves filled with miscellaneous tools. Wheelbarrows line the walls, burlap bags, sugar, rope and rum bottles are stored throughout.

The Menacing Laborer 1 picks through the tools and rope and fills his bag. Menacing Laborers 2 and 3 greedily pack rum bottles into burlap bags.

> **MARY**
> You might need other things besides rum.

> **MENACING LABORER 2**
> This is so we can burn more.

Menacing Laborer 1 gives them a stern look. They pack other useful items into burlap bags and leave in a hurry.

Himmelman turns to Mary, while rubbing his wrists.

> **HIMMELMAN**
> Juju?

> **MARY**
> My dog when I was little.

Himmelman smiles.

—STUDY

> **HIMMELMAN**
> Let's go have a drink to Juju and the Obeah
> woman.

Mary sits across from Himmelman. Himmelman rests on the edge of his desk. He takes her empty glass and places it on his desk.

> **HIMMELMAN (CONT'D)**
> What brings you out here tonight?

> **MARY**
> I need your help to rescue a friend.

> **HIMMELMAN**
> From where?

> **MARY**
> Griffith has him.

> **HIMMELMAN**
> Even if I did not owe you my life, that is a good enough reason for me to help. I never did like that man.

> **MARY**
> That makes two of us.

RAPPING on the window. They turn to see the smiling face of Axeline.

> **MARY (CONT'D)**
> Axeline?

> **HIMMELMAN**
> I'm not used to having beautiful women visit me in the middle of the night like this.

Himmelman and Mary go to the window.

SMASH. They jump and turn to see the study door being kicked open by Griffith's armed men. Axeline drops out of sight. Griffiths enters.

> **GRIFFITH**
> This has turned out to be such a lucky night for me. I came because of a hunch that you might be harboring Negroes and I find a celebration in progress. Mind if I join in?

Griffith picks up one of the glasses from the desk and pours himself a drink.

> **GRIFFITH (CONT'D)**
> You just had to mess with the natural order of things...
> *(to the armed men)*
> Tie them up!

The armed men bind Himmelman's and Mary's hand and feet. They pour kerosene throughout the building.

> **GRIFFITH (CONT'D)**
> *(to Himmelman)*
> What a sad turn of events that these nigger animals had to burn down the sugar factory...with you in it.

Griffith chugs his drink and throws the glass against the wall.

> **GRIFFITH (CONT'D)**
> I am really going to miss this place.

WILL
Should we leave her too?

GRIFFITH
Bring her. She is going to put an end to what she started.

Will hits Himmelman on the head with the butt of his gun. Himmelman's body goes limp. An open wound on his head oozes blood. Two armed men pull Mary out of the study and Griffith strolls behind.

—COURTYARD

Mary lies on the floor of Griffith's carriage, struggling to untie herself.

The armed men pour kerosene on the exterior of the factory and storage shack.

Griffith savors a cigar as he watches the men. The armed men finish and Griffith flicks his lit cigar butt onto the kerosene soaked building. The factory is consumed in flames.

Griffith and his men leave. Griffith in the carriage and his men on horses.

Axeline runs to the front door and approaches the flames. She retreats and runs back to the study window. She looks through and spots Himmelman's still body on the floor. The flames enter the study and quickly grow.

Axeline frantically looks around the ground and spots a large stick. She runs to the window and SMASHES it several times, being careful to remove jagged edges. She climbs through the window and enters the smoke filled, study.

Axeline covers her nose and COUGHS. She fans the smoke with her free hand and rushes over to Himmelman. She unties him and shakes his shoulder.

> **AXELINE**
> Wake up!

Himmelman does not respond. Axeline grabs his arm and struggles to drag him a few feet. His head hits the side of a coffee table.

> **AXELINE (CONT'D)**
> Sorry!

Himmelman's eyes open groggily and he looks up at the smoke filled room.

> **HIMMELMAN**
> So many clouds. I'm in heaven.

He reaches for Axeline's face and touches it.

> **HIMMELMAN (CONT'D)**
> Angel?

Axeline blushes.

A flaming ceiling beam CRASHES a few feet away from them. Axeline SCREAMS and Himmelman comes out of his daze. He sits up quickly and rubs his head.

> **HIMMELMAN (CONT'D)**
> Dammit, Griffith!

EXPLOSIONS heard throughout the factory.

Himmelman grabs Axeline's hand and runs with her to the window. He assists as she scrambles out. He follows. They escape in time to see the roof of the factory collapse.

They watch the burning building for a few moments.

Himmelman WHISTLES and a few moments later a horse GALLOPS toward him and stops in front of him.

Himmelman nuzzles the horse and pats its head.

Himmelman lifts Axeline onto the horse. He mounts the horse and sits in front of Axeline. He gently prods the horse with his heels and the horse TROTS along.

> **HIMMELMAN (CONT'D)**
> You'd better hold on tight.

Axeline moves in closer and holds him tightly. Himmelman prods and the horse bursts into a GALLOP.

EXT./INT. ESTATE GRIFFITH—STABLE—NIGHT

Griffith arrives and is met by several of his armed men. Mary glares at Griffith.

> **GRIFFITH**
> Throw her in the stable. I'll be back.

Griffith walks to his house.

The armed men drag Mary into the dark stable and leave her. Will and Jack stand guard. Jack pulls a harmonica from his pocket and plays. The melodious SOUND fills the air. Will sits on a bale of hay and closes his eyes.

Mary looks around and tries to untie the ropes. MOVEMENT. Mary WHISPERS.

MARY

Singer, is that you?

SINGER

Mary?

A bound Mary squirms her way closer to Singer, who is chained to the wall. Singer, bruised and bloody, grimaces as he sits up. Mary sits next to him and leans her head on his shoulder, he rests his head on hers.

MARY

I'm so sorry...

SINGER

Shhh, it's okay.

MARY

I didn't think I'd ever see you again.

SINGER

Me neither. I wish you weren't here though.

MARY

I'd rather be here with you than anywhere else.

Singer tries to make light of their situation.

SINGER

And I'd rather be with you anywhere else than here.

MARY
(Smiling)

That would be better.

SINGER

When I thought of spending the rest of my life with you, I imagined having a few years with you, not minutes or hours.

MARY

The key to happiness is being content with what you have.

Singer lifts his head excitedly.

SINGER

The key! That's it. He left it on the table.

Mary squirms over to the table and struggles to stand, but is unable. As Mary continues her efforts to stand, she accidentally hits the table and the knives fall onto her, cushioning the sound to a soft THUD, but barely avoiding cutting her. She flinches.

Jack stops playing his harmonica and looks at the stable door suspiciously. Will's eyes are still closed.

JACK

What was that? Wake up! Did you hear something?

Will jumps and opens his eyes.

WILL

What? Probably, just the horses.

JACK

Go check! I checked the bedroom last time. Now it's your turn to check something.

Will does not budge.

WILL

(laughing)

I'm afraid, maybe the perfume monster is in there.

JACK

I guess I'll just have to tell the boss that you were sleeping on the job.

Will gets up.

WILL

I'm only doing this because I need to stretch.

Will opens the stable door and peers into the room as Jack looks on expectantly.

Singer immediately pulls on his chains noisily, as though trying to escape. Mary lies quietly, out of view.

From the doorway, Will looks at the struggling Singer.

WILL (CONT'D)

That's not going to help. You might as well save your strength.

Will turns and closes the door.

WILL (CONT'D)

No perfume monsters in there.

Jack ignores him and plays his harmonica. Will returns to his seated position and closes his eyes.

Mary listens for a few seconds and springs into action. She uses one of the knives to cut the rope from her wrists and legs. She retrieves the keys for Singer's chains off the table, runs over to him and unlocks his chains.

Mary looks around and heads to the window. Singer gently pulls her back and holds her tenderly. He kisses her passionately and she responds.

> **SINGER**
>> Now we can go.

They run to the window. Singer quietly opens it, helps Mary out and follows.

They hurriedly leave the stable area and head toward the road.

Griffith approaches the stable. Jack stops playing the harmonica and nudges Will. Will's eyes remain closed as he brushes away Jack's hand.

> **GRIFFITH**
>> *(to Will)*
>> I'm not paying you to sleep!

Jack jumps and stands at attention.

> **WILL**
>> Just checked on the prisoners, sir. All is well.

Jack opens the stable door for Griffith. Griffith enters, Will and Jack follow.

Griffith looks around the empty stable and stares at the open window.

GRIFFITH
Dammit!

WILL
They were just here, sir!

GRIFFITH
You incompetent idiots. Get my dogs, now! If you do not catch them, I will have both of your heads tonight.

Will and Jack scramble out of the stable.

Griffith eyes the cut ropes that held Mary. He angrily flips the wooden table over and storms out of the stable.

EXT. DIRT ROAD—NIGHT

Dogs BARK in the distance. Mary and Singer look back in the direction of the barking. A pack of dogs, followed by Griffith and his army, rush toward them.

Mary and Singer run into the sugar cane fields. The dogs and men pursue and gain distance quickly.

Mary's dress gets caught in the thicket and she falls, Singer stops and helps her.

Singer pulls a knife from his pocket and cuts Mary free. He helps her to her feet. The dogs surround them and GROWL. Singer holds Mary protectively. Griffith and his men saunter over to them.

EXT. STABLE—NIGHT

Will stands at attention outside the stable. CRUNCH of twigs. He peers into the darkness. Axeline steps from behind the shadows and smiles coyly.

>   **WILL**
>   Hey, what's going on?

Will, with gun in hand, leaves his post and approaches Axeline.

>   **AXELINE**
>   Please don't shoot. I don't want to fight.

Will grabs Axeline roughly and squeezes her butt.

>   **WILL**
>   Well maybe I like a good fight.

Axeline struggles with him briefly before Himmelman charges from behind a tree and hits Will on the head with his gun, knocking him unconscious.

>   **HIMMELMAN**
>   Grab his gun.

Axeline gingerly touches the gun.

>   **HIMMELMAN (CONT'D)**
>   Have you ever fired one of those before?

>   **AXELINE**
>   No.

Himmelman stands behind Axeline, positions the gun in her hands and gives her a quick shooting lesson.

HIMMELMAN
Just point it at whatever you want to shoot and pull back on this thing here.

Axeline answers dubiously.

AXELINE
Okay.

HIMMELMAN
Just look like you know what you're doing and you may not even have to fire it.

INT. STABLE—NIGHT

Singer, clothed only in his britches, is bound and lying on the table. Beads of sweat drip from his head. Griffith holds the knife over Singer's crotch.

Mary's hands are tied. Jack positions her next to the table. Mary squeezes her eyes shut and turns her head.

GRIFFITH
(to Mary)

Open your eyes. If you don't, I will make it more painful for him.

Mary opens her eyes and looks at Singer.

GRIFFITH (CONT'D)
That's right.

Angela Golden Bryan

Griffith takes his knife and RIPS Singer's pants open. Singer GASPS. Mary SCREAMS.

MARY
No!

Griffith LAUGHS.

GRIFFITH
You two are so excitable.

Griffith reaches and pulls at Singer's pants. SMASH. The door bursts open.

Himmelman and Axeline rush inside, guns raised. Griffith and Jack spin around and face them.

HIMMELMAN
Both of you, hands up!

Griffith slowly raises his hands. Jack reaches for his gun. BANG. Axeline shoots the gun out of Jack's hand.

HIMMELMAN (CONT'D)
Impressive!

AXELINE
I was aiming for his head.

Will rushes in, out of breath and rubbing his head. Jack grabs his gun from the floor.

JACK
(to Himmelman and Axeline)
You and you, put down those guns!

GRIFFITH
(*to Will*)
It took you long enough.

WILL
Hundreds of them are coming...

GRIFFITH
I have had enough of your incompetence for one day!

Griffith shoots and Will drops. Jack runs to Will's side.

GRIFFITH (CONT'D)
Now, as I was saying...

The saddles on the wall shake, the ground quakes and POUNDING sounds on the ground.

A sea of quickly approaching torch lights floods the grounds. Everyone turns to look out the door. Jack assists Will as they hurry off, unnoticed.

GRIFFITH (CONT'D)
What in the name of...?

Griffith walks to the door, his eyes wide.

An army of black bodies, many with torches, STAMPEDE the grounds, reaching the stable in seconds. They carry axes, machetes, pitchforks and shovels.

Griffith, alone, steps out of the stable and is overtaken by the sea of laborers.

Lewis walks into the stable.

HIMMELMAN
What took you so long?

SINGER
Lewis?

Lewis walks over to Singer and unties him.

LEWIS
You look surprised to see me.

SINGER
I never expected …

LEWIS
Blood is thicker than water, even if it is half-blood. Besides, we agreed – for our momma…

SINGER
For momma.

Himmelman removes the rope from Mary. Axeline wields her gun proudly. Himmelman gently lowers her hand and gun.

HIMMELMAN
Lewis has been going to the plantations and the free gut neighborhoods, ever since day one, assembling an army.

LEWIS
Just taking care of business.

Lewis moves closer to Mary. Singer smoothly takes Mary's hand and holds it. Lewis looks at their hands and then at them. Mary looks at Lewis apologetically. Lewis addresses Singer.

LEWIS (CONT'D)

If you hurt her, I'll kill you.

The SHOUTING of the laborers outside the stable intensifies. Himmelman, Axeline, Lewis, Singer and Mary exit and walk into the sea of bodies. They press through to where Griffith is kneeling. The crowd quiets. Griffith looks up and spots Lewis.

GRIFFITH

Thank God, it's you Lewis. Tell them who I am.

Lewis steps forward.

LEWIS

Yes, sir.

Lewis rests his hand on Griffith's shoulder.

LEWIS (CONT'D)

This is Mr. Griffith and we need to give him special treatment.

Griffith relaxes.

LEWIS (CONT'D)

He owns this plantation and he is one of the meanest men alive. He rapes our women and beats us. He forces us to work for almost nothing and he does not honor Contract Day.

Griffith's face fills with horror. Lewis walks away. The laborers move in ominously. Griffith SCREAMS. SOUND of machetes, shovels and axes tearing into flesh.

Lewis joins Mary and Singer as they mount horses.

EXT. ESTATE ANNA'S HOPE—GROUNDS—DAWN

A rooster CROWS. Elderly, injured, and female laborers with small children prepare to leave for the country. A mother CRIES. A toddler clings to his father's leg.

Susanna, Cy, Martha, Tilda and her family rouse.

> **SUSANNA**
> Has anybody seen Axeline?

> **MARTHA**
> Not since last night.

> **SUSANNA**
> I have to fight, but I refuse to go with that idiot Jonas!

> **TILDA**
> I'll wait here with you until Mary comes back. I'm sure Axeline won't be far behind her.

Tilda hugs her father and kisses his cheek. She turns to her mother and hugs her more gently.

> **TILDA (CONT'D)**
> Don't worry, mommy. I'll be fine.

Tilda's mother looks at her with concern. Tilda hugs her brother and sister.

Jonas rallies the laborers. The Three Menacing Laborers listen intently.

JONAS
Today we burn and tear down anything or anyone that gets in our way!

MENACING LABORER 1
But Mary isn't here yet.

JONAS
What has she to do with me?

MENACING LABORER 1
She said you were a fine leader. I thought you were fighting together.

Jonas LAUGHS.

JONAS
Mary and her tricks! Unless a miracle happens, she won't be back. We leave in 10 minutes!

The Menacing Laborers look at each other in confusion.

Cy is perched atop a tree, peering into the distance. He squints for a few seconds and then becomes excited. He scrambles down and runs to Susanna, Martha, Tilda and her family.

CY
Come. Come see.

MARTHA
What is it?

Sound of MARCHING in a distance. The laborers take notice and face the direction of the sound.

SUSANNA
What in the world is going on?

A massive army of laborers approaches. Mary, Singer, Axeline and Lewis are on horses leading them.

Susanna LAUGHS heartily.

SUSANNA (CONT'D)
She did it!

Mary, Cy, Singer, Axeline and Lewis, along with the massive army enter the grounds of Estate Anna's Hope.

Jonas approaches Mary. The Menacing Laborers follow. They stop in front her.

MARY
I'm not looking for trouble. I'm here to get my friends.

Jonas motions to Mary's army.

JONAS
You have proven yourself.

Jonas extends his hand to Mary and they shake hands. Mary gives a SPEECH to the crowd that has gathered.

MARY
My friends, let us join hands in battle as brothers and sisters. Let us fight not just for today, but for

tomorrow and for our families and our family's families. Let us fight for justice and dignity!

The crowd CHEERS.

> **MARY (CONT'D)**
> And for these we must also be willing to die. Who's with me?

The crowd CHEERS wildly as Mary raises a torch.

> **MARY (CONT'D)**
> Fireburn!

The crowd CHANTS "Fireburn!"

EXT. CHRISTIANSTED–HARBOR–DAY

Danish military ships are docked. Armed Danish soldiers disembark hurriedly and march inland.

EXT./INT. CHRISTIANSTED—GOVERNMENT HOUSE —DAY

Armed Danish soldiers stand at attention.

—GOVERNOR'S OFFICE

Governor Garde reclines in his chair and smokes his pipe. The commander gives his report while the lieutenant governor and aides listen.

> **COMMANDER OF THE FORT**
> We can only anticipate that more burning and looting will occur until we put an end to it.

GOVERNOR GARDE
Yes, yes, do not bore me with the details.

COMMANDER OF THE FORT
Yes, sir.

GOVERNOR GARDE
We will have a public execution so that the Negroes can understand who they're dealing with. We will start with Mary and end with a gala the island has never seen.

COMMANDER OF THE FORT
Sir, now is not the time to plan a party.

GOVERNOR GARDE
If you had been more aggressive in the beginning, like I said, things would not have progressed this far and I would not need to be planning a gala to boost the morale!

COMMANDER OF THE FORT
Sir?

GOVERNOR GARDE
You heard me! Carry out my orders and let's put an end to this.

COMMANDER OF THE FORT
Yes, sir.

The commander turns to leave.

GOVERNOR GARDE
Commander?

COMMANDER OF THE FORT
Yes, sir?

GOVERNOR GARDE
Did the Negroes burn the rum factory?

COMMANDER OF THE FORT
Yes, sir.

GOVERNOR GARDE
Dammit!

The governor tenses in his seat and smashes his pipe down on his desk. The commander leaves the governor's office and MUTTERS under his breath.

COMMANDER OF THE FORT
Idiot!

EXT. JUST WEST OF ESTATE ANNA'S HOPE—DUSK

Mary, Singer, Lewis, Susanna, Axeline, Tilda, Jonas and Menacing Laborers 1, 2 and 3 and the massive army are armed with unlit torches, machetes, shovels, pitchforks and pickaxes.

MARY
Torches ready? We burn everything in our path, all the way to Bassin jail house!

Everyone with torches raises them.

Mary lights one of her torches. Everyone with torches follows suit and passes the light.

> **MARY (CONT'D)**
> Let's go!

The massive army charges forward. Menacing Laborers 1, 2 and 3 take the lead.

They approach Estate Peter's Rest with its looming crushing station.

Menacing Laborer 1 extends his hand to throw one of his torches. Just as he releases. BANG.

A shot rings out from a rooftop and Menacing Laborer 1 drops, blood pouring from a chest wound. His torch falls a few feet away.

SHOTS ring out from the rooftops.

> **MARY**
> Pull back! Pull back!

The laborers retreat. Danish soldiers come from behind buildings and surround the laborers. They attack the laborers with bayonets, rifles and clubs. The laborers engage in battle with their work tools and torches.

Mary fires her last shot in her gun and throws the gun down. She wields her machete and fights a soldier, the soldier gains the upper hand and raises his bayonet to stab Mary.

Jonas stabs the soldier in the back and the soldier drops.

Jonas grabs Mary's arm and pulls her along as they run.

> **JONAS**
> They've got your friend! Come.

Mary is concerned and follows willingly.

>   **MARY**
> Who?

>   **JONAS**
> The one whose mouth don't have no Sunday.

>   **MARY**
> Susanna?

>   **JONAS**
> Yes.

Jonas quickly leads Mary to the stables. Four soldiers await. Mary turns in shock. Jonas pushes Mary toward them.

>   **JONAS (CONT'D)**
> Here she is. As promised.

>   **DANISH SOLDIER 1**
> And you will have safe passage back to Antigua, as promised…

Jonas smiles wickedly at Mary and turns to leave. Danish Soldier 2 shoots Jonas in the back and Jonas drops.

>   **DANISH SOLDIER 1 (CONT'D)**
> …in a box.

The Danish soldiers LAUGH. Danish Soldier 1 hits Mary over the head with the butt of his rifle and she collapses.

They carry Mary off.

The fight continues between the laborers and the Danish army. It is a losing battle for the laborers.

Singer looks frantically for Mary and calls for the remaining laborers to retreat. He does not find Mary, but finds her blood-stained kerchief, and Buddhoe's earring. He stares at it for a moment, attaches the earring to the scarf and then sticks it in his pocket. He heads back to where the others continue fighting. Lewis, assisting the laborers, points them to various hiding places, checks the wounded. The laborers, as instructed, retreat hastily. Many lay dead.

INT. CHRISTIANSTED— BASSIN JAIL HOUSE PRISON CELL—NIGHT

Cramped. Dirty. A wooden cot with tattered and filthy mattress.

Mary lies motionless on the cot. Blood oozes from a cut on her head. She is dirty and bloody.

EXT. CHRISTIANSTED—GALLOWS BAY—DAY

A row of gallows stand ominously. Soldiers patrol the streets. Sound of POUNDING as a workman nails the base of one of the gallows.

INT. CHRISTIANSTED—BASSIN JAIL HOUSE PRISON CELL—DAY

One room with desk and chair. Opposite is a tiny cell. Light from window streams in.

Mary lies on the cot, staring blankly at the ceiling. The prison guard slouches on the chair, arms crossed, with feet on desk. He leans over and spits into a small pail next to his desk. He wipes his mouth with the back of his hand.

PRISON GUARD

Don't you want to look out the window and see the surprise they're building for you and your little friends? I was in favor of the firing squad...so much more dignified.

Mary does not answer.

PRISON GUARD (CONT'D)

You'll see soon enough.

INT. GOVERNOR'S OFFICE—DAY

Governor Garde looks out the window. Gallows Bay is in the distance. His lieutenant governor briefs him.

LT. GOVERNOR

Laborers are back to work, with over 400 arrests, 100 dead, 12 executed and 39 death sentences.

GOVERNOR GARDE

How did we fair?

LT. GOVERNOR

We lost two soldiers and one plantation owner.

GOVERNOR GARDE

And the Negresses?

LT. GOVERNOR

Per your request they have been imprisoned and await public execution. But, sir, there is an urgent issue that needs to be addressed.

GOVERNOR GARDE
No more discussions!

LT. GOVERNOR
But, sir...

GOVERNOR GARDE
Have my driver prepare my carriage—now!

LT. GOVERNOR
Yes, sir.

The lieutenant governor exits.

EXT. CHRISTIANSTED—GALLOWS BAY—DAY

Crowded with laborers and Whites, segregated. Armed soldiers patrol. Four empty gallows.

A carriage arrives. Soldiers pull Susanna, Axeline and Tilda out. The women are dirty and battered and their hands are tied. WHISPERING and pointing at them from the Whites. A little white boy picks up a stone and throws it at Susanna. His mother smiles proudly at him.

The governor's carriage arrives and he is escorted to a covered viewing stand where other high ranking officials are in place. The white women fan themselves with lace fans.

The soldiers take Susanna, Axeline and Tilda to the gallows and help each of them on a stool and place a noose around their necks. One spot under one of the nooses is vacant. A minister, holds a Bible and stands to the side.

The governor looks at the empty spot, takes a time piece from his pocket and looks at it impatiently.

A carriage careens around the bend, coming to a quick stop, barely missing a passerby. The driver jumps off the carriage and opens the door for the prison guard. Mary is bound and glares at him with hatred. One of her eyes is swollen, bruised and half-closed.

The guard has a fresh scratch on his face that he blots with a bloody handkerchief before putting it in his pocket. He bends over, cuts the rope on Mary's hand and feet and pulls her out of the carriage.

People in the crowd turn and stare as the guard drags Mary to the gallows. Cy and Martha are in the crowd, along with Tilda's Father. Tilda's father stares at her sadly. Cy spots Mary.

CY
Mommy, it's...

Martha quickly covers Cy's mouth with her hand.

Mary is shoved onto the stool and the noose is placed around her neck.

GOVERNOR GARDE
(sarcastically)
Now that our guest of honor is here we may proceed.

LAUGHS from the Whites in the crowd.

GOVERNOR GARDE (CONT'D)
We are here today to stand united in the face of disaster caused by these women and their followers. Let us proceed with justice.

CHEERS of approval from the Whites.

GOVERNOR GARDE (CONT'D)
Minister, please pray over these lost souls.

The minister approaches the women, opens his Bible and READS the 23rd Psalm.

Sound of GALLOPING. Heads turn. Singer drives a horse and carriage. The carriage stops sharply. Singer jumps down and helps Himmelman out.

Himmelman hurriedly approaches the governor. The crowd stares. MURMURS.

HIMMELMAN
Most Honorable Governor Garde.

GOVERNOR GARDE
Whatever it is can wait, Mr. Himmelman. I am in the middle of official business.

HIMMELMAN
Since when has the execution of women been legal, sir?

GOVERNOR GARDE
I beg your pardon?

HIMMELMAN
It is illegal to execute women in the Danish West Indies. These women deserve a fair trial.

GOVERNOR'S WIFE
They are not women, they're animals!

The Whites in the crowd CHANT "Animals, animals, animals!" They are silenced by Himmelman.

HIMMELMAN
Please forgive my impertinence, genteel ladies and most respected gentlemen, but if this is true, many of the men here are guilty of bestiality and the light skinned children on your plantations testify to this reprehensible sin.

GASPS from several white women. A white woman in the crowd faints. Several white women fan her and give her smelling salts. Several men in the crowd look embarrassed.

The governor turns red and looks guiltily at a well-dressed light skinned black woman and her two mullato children in the crowd.

The governor's wife follows his gaze and hatred fills her eyes.

The governor's wife lifts her skirt, turns and leaves in a huff. The governor looks on helplessly.

The lieutenant governor approaches the governor. They WHISPER.

LT. GOVERNOR
He's right, sir.

GOVERNOR GARDE
Why was I not informed of this before?

LT. GOVERNOR
You said you did not want to discuss it further, sir.

GOVERNOR GARDE
You incompetent idiot! I will have your head when we are done here.

The flustered governor steps forward.

GOVERNOR GARDE (CONT'D)
Ladies and gentlemen. By the power vested in me, as governor of these Danish West Indies, I hereby grant these four ladies the opportunity to have a trial.

Disapproving MUTTERING from the Whites. The governor turns and faces the Blacks.

GOVERNOR GARDE (CONT'D)
And may the outcome of the trial serve as a deterrent to any of you that would think to create unrest in these islands in the future!

The governor storms off and the Whites follow. The laborers CHEER enthusiastically.

The soldiers remove the nooses from the Susanna, Axeline and Tilda's necks and lead them away.

Martha cries as she holds Cy close. The crowd's CHEERING softens. Tilda's father mournfully follows the soldier as he leads Mary, Susanna, Axeline and Tilda away.

Mary and the other women pass by Himmelman and Singer. Himmelman addresses Mary and the others apologetically.

HIMMELMAN
It's the best I could do.

MARY
You're a good man.

Mary and Singer's eyes meet. The soldier looks at them. Mary turns her gaze and looks blindly ahead. Singer stares after her sadly. He pulls her kerchief from his pocket, Buddhoe's earring hanging from it.

INT. COURT ROOM—DAY–YEAR 1882

Judge sitting at his desk. Mary, Susanna, Axeline and Tilda stand before the judge emotionless as their charges are read, their hands bound.

JUDGE
I find the defendants Mary Thomas, Susanna Abrahamsen, Axeline Salomon and Matilda McBean guilty. I hereby sentence you each to hard labor, for life, for orchestrating and leading the arson rebellion of 1878. Your sentence will be served in the Copenhagen Women's Penitentiary.

EXT. STABLE—DAY–YEAR 1898

Singer, worn in appearance, looks on as young stable hands tend to horses. He makes notes in a small notebook and puts it in his pants pocket.

He walks to the front of the building to find an older Lewis accepting money from a man who turns and leaves with a horse. As the man leaves, the brothers head back inside the stable. A sign reads "TWO BROTHERS STABLE AND CARRIAGE SALES".

EXT. DENMARK—COPENHAGEN WOMEN'S PENITENTIARY—DAY

Open, fenced in area. Armed guards patrol the grounds. Uniformed female prisoners dig ditches and perform various tasks. Among the prisoners are Mary, Susanna, Tilda and Axeline.

A prison guard approaches and beckons for the four women to come.

PRISON GUARD
Komme.

EXT. SHIP "THEA"—OFF THE COAST OF ST. CROIX, DANISH WEST INDIES—DAY

Large ship. Wooden deck scattered with white passengers who excitedly point to the island in the distance.

Mary, Susanna, Axeline and Tilda in plain clothes are off to the side by themselves, peacefully watching the approaching shoreline of St. Croix.

A majestic bird soars overhead. Mary looks up and smiles.

THE END

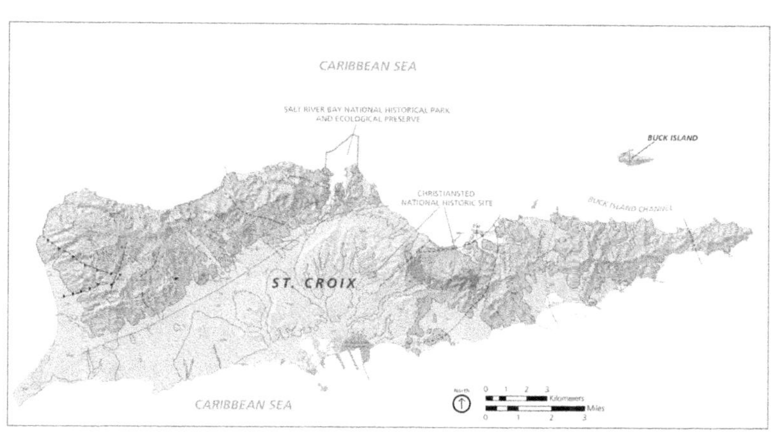

CARIBBEAN SEA
SALT RIVER BAY NATIONAL HISTORICAL PARK
AND ECOLOGICAL PRESERVE
BUCK ISLAND
CHRISTIANSTED
NATIONAL HISTORIC SITE
BUCK ISLAND CHANNEL
ST. CROIX
CARIBBEAN SEA
North
Kilometers
Miles
0   1   2   3
0   1   2   3

PART 4

EPILOGUE

Although sentenced to hard labor for life, the four women did not serve their full sentences in Denmark. Upon returning to the Danish West Indies, Mary Thomas reportedly got married and had a son. Some believe that prior to the Fireburn, she had three children and had not wed. Mary died on March 16, 1905, and is buried in the Estate Williams Delight cemetery. Susanna died on July 20, 1906, while incarcerated at the Richmond jail in Christiansted, and is buried in the adjacent cemetery.

Mathilde died at the age of 78 on October 10, 1935, at Estate Hogensborg, and is buried in the Frederiksted cemetery. Information regarding Axeline's death has not surfaced yet.

Although all of the women are referred to as "Queens," and each was a leader of the Fireburn, it is Mary Thomas that remains the most popular, or notorious. Some view her as a "trouble-making drunk" while others refer to her affectionately as the heroine, "Queen Mary."

Whether the four queens were villains or foes, Fireburn was an historic event which helped reform the labor laws of the islands. The Labor Law of 1849 was repealed on October 24, 1879, which meant that laborers could travel between estates, as well as off-island, and freely seek employment.

Some say that because of the economic, social, and political changes that resulted from the Fireburn, the Fireburn is the true emancipation date of the Danish West Indies. The Fireburn forced the European leadership to acknowledge the rights of the workers and, as a result, change did come.

The United States purchased the Danish West Indies in March of 1917, and renamed the islands "U.S. Virgin Islands." They are still U.S. territory and each year many islanders commemorate Fireburn on the first of October, which was the original date for Contract Day.

Queen Mary Folksong

Queen Mary, oh where you gon' go burn?
Queen Mary oh where you gon' go burn?
Don't ask me nothin' at all. Just give me the match and oil.
Bassin Jailhouse, ah there the money there.
Don't ask me nothin' at all. Just give me the match and oil.
Bassin Jailhouse, ah there the money there.
Queen Mary, oh where you gon' go burn?
Queen Mary, oh where you gon' go burn?
Don't ask me nothin' at all. Just give me the match and
trash. Bassin Jailhouse, ah there the money there.
Don't ask me nothin' at all. Just give me the match and
trash. Bassin Jailhouse, ah there the money there.
We gon' burn Bassin come down,
And when we reach the factory, we'll burn am level down.

While the author of the "Queen Mary" folk song is unknown, most islanders (at least the old-timers) know the words and sing it in celebration of the four queens of the 1878 Fireburn and the queens' contributions to labor reform. The song has several variations, as it has changed when passed down through generations. Pass it on!

Acknowledgments

Special thanks go to a number of people, without whom this book would not be possible.

Thank you, Mom and Dad for the gift of being raised on beautiful St. Croix, and for your encouragement and excitement regarding my writing *Fireburn* despite how long it took me.

Thank you, Ken, my husband, my rock – I really could not have done this without your support. To Kenny, my son – thank you for helping me to see things in black and white. And to Erin, my daughter – thank you for helping me to see things in vibrant colors. Each of you helps me to stay balanced.

Thank you to my storytelling aunts on both sides of my family: Gerda, Jenny and Gloria – your stories inspired me to tell my own.

Thank you, the Honorable Myron D. Jackson, for taking the time to read my screenplay and provide me with valuable feedback. I appreciate your foreword and your encouragement to "go back and fetch it."

Thank you, Fireburn expert, Wayne James, for allowing me to "pick your brain" as far back as 2010, and for setting the record straight concerning the number of queens involved in the Fireburn.

Thanks to my screenwriting coach, Rolando Vinas, who helped get the ball rolling by patiently coaching me on how to get *Fireburn* out of my heart and onto paper.

Thank you to Allison Daigle, artist, for capturing my vision so beautifully.

Thank you to my publisher, Barbara Dee, for pulling it all together and encouraging me at every step.

About the Author

Angela Golden Bryan, an acclaimed storyteller and actress, grew up on the beautiful island of St. Croix, U.S. Virgin Islands, in a culture rich in oral tradition. She experienced what are still long-held traditions today, including the recitation of folktales in homes and at family gatherings, and more formal poetic recitations in schools and churches.

As a child, she listened in fascination to stories about Anansi, the mischievous spider; became "scared to death" by the goatfoot woman; and was amazed at the bravery of her great-great-grandmother, Moriah, who took part in the history-making event, Fireburn.

Eventually, Bryan became the one to tell the stories to her family, and later to her own children. Naturally, she always dreamed of sharing the St. Croix "Fireburn" story with all of her extended family, community, country, and beyond.

After moving from St. Croix, she lived in Illinois, southern California, southern Spain, and Hawaii. She earned her Master of Science degree in Counseling Psychology while serving in the U.S. Navy, and also holds a Master of Practical Theology from Wesley Seminary.

In her career, Bryan was able to combine her love for entertaining and storytelling to excel as an actress. She has over 20 years of experience in television, film, theater, voice-overs and commercials. Bryan is an "edutainer" –a keynote speaker who provides education and inspiration in an entertaining manner, and is a certified speaker, trainer and coach with the John Maxwell team. She has written for the internationally published devotionals, *Light from the Word* and *Vista.*

Bryan settled down in South Florida where she lives with her husband. They both look forward to visits from their two adult "children" as well as traveling, and returning to visit her beloved islands whenever possible.

Angela Golden Bryan

Photography (also back cover photo) by Derek Latta.

www.ingramcontent.com/pod-product-compliance
Lightning Source LLC
Chambersburg PA
CBHW070950180726
48291CB00004B/1231